SKUNK: A LIFE

by Peter Aleshkovsky

Peter Aleshkovsky was born in 1957 in Moscow.
An archaeologist by training, he spent many years
restoring monasteries in Northern Russia.
He is the author of *Stargorod,*
a cycle of 30 narratives about provincial Russia,
and three other novels: *Seagull, Vladimir Chigrintsev*
(a neo-gothic novel shortlisted for the 1996
Booker Russian Novel Prize, see excerpt in Glas 16),
and *Harlequin* (about 18th-century poet Trediakovsky).
Skunk: a Life was shortlisted for
the Booker Russian Novel Prize in 1994.

Arch Tait is senior lecturer at
the Department of Russian Literature,
University of Birmingham,
and the UK editor of Glas New Russian Writing.

Glas New Russian Writing

a book series of contemporary Russian writing
edited by Natasha Perova & Arch Tait

volume 15

Back issues of Glas:

REVOLUTION
SOVIET GROTESQUE
WOMEN'S VIEW
LOVE & FEAR
BULGAKOV & MANDELSTAM
JEWS & STRANGERS
BOOKER WINNERS & OTHERS
LOVE RUSSIAN STYLE
THE SCARED GENERATION
BOOKER WINNERS & OTHERS – II
CAPTIVES
FROM THREE WORLDS
A WILL & A WAY
BEYOND THE LOOKING-GLAS

Glas New Russian Writing

PETER ALESHKOVSKY

SKUNK: A LIFE

TRANSLATED BY ARCH TAIT

glas

GLAS Publishers (Russia)
Moscow 119517, P.O.Box 47, Russia
Tel/Fax: +7-095-441 9157
Email: perova@glas.msk.su

GLAS Publishers (UK)
Dept. of Russian Literature,
University of Birmingham
Birmingham, B15 2TT, UK
Tel/Fax: +44(0)121-414 6047
Email: a.l.tait@bham.ac.uk

Cover design by Mikhail Molochnikov
Front cover photograph by Igor Mukhin
Inside: details from Sergei Potapov's series of etchings "Perestroika"
Camera-ready copy by Tatiana Shaposhnikova

First publication in English
First published in Russian in *Druzhba Narodov* № 7, 1993

Glas gratefully acknowledges the financial and moral support
of the Arts Council of England and the Fund for Central and
East European Book Projects, Amsterdam

ISBN 5-7172-0033-1

Skunk: a Life

Part One

1

It was not so many years ago, but neither was it the day before yesterday, in times when Stargorod still abounded in witty townsfolk of a merry disposition, that a cracking frost drove a gregarious company of men of diverse ages off the street and into the store room of a vegetable shop which, in the era before historical materialism, had served the city as the sentry post on the main St Petersburg highway. The room was divided off from the main storage area by a partition of sturdy alder plywood and supplied with a rudimentary pine table and benches daubed with brown ship's paint in place of varnish. The one and only barred window was covered with a cheery tracery of frost, and in the corner blazed a stove fashioned from a forty-gallon petrol tank.

The room was warm and stuffy. When all had settled themselves to their satisfaction, and shed their overcoats and quilted jackets, the gathering resolved to power down the rest of the shop an hour before the advertized closing time, bolt the door, and unwind with a classic of fortified wines, *Three Sevens*, which was conveniently to hand on the shop's shelves; to offset its fulsome body they judiciously selected curly soused cucumbers and pickled cabbage from the barrel.

There were three lady shop assistants to minister to these five refugees from winter's thrall and their own lonely hearts. The ladies were without husbands and were, firstly, Anna Ivanovna, the shop's manageress and a woman who had seen much of life; secondly, Raissa, considerably younger, in fact only about thirty, a singer of songs and teller of tales; and finally Zoika Khoryova, younger still, just eighteen years of age but already eight months pregnant, and hence not in contention.

And if one old fellow who was pushing fifty, a pint-sized Casanova full of life, wit and zest, did, after just one tumbler of *Three Sevens*, propose unsubtly to Zoika that he should slip her half a length, the manageress, defending the interests of her expectant colleague, tut-tutted the reprobate so maternally that everybody, appreciating the humour of the situation, fell about with joyful mirth.

Before long a conversation about politics struck up in one of the corners between some sad old guys no longer fit for anything better, while two somewhat younger heartthrobs moved in on Anna Ivanovna and Raissa.

A general libation to the uniquely moving toast, "May God grant it's not our last!", instantly created that amazing mood so beloved of simple Russian folk. With the passage of some half an hour they were crooning "The frost, the frost..." at the ladies' end of the table. Where political controversy had seemed about to flare the picture was different: the less resistant of the disputants was now asleep nose down on the table; the second had gone outside to relieve himself and was gazing raptly at the moon, wholly unable to terminate his meditation. Swaying slightly and trying in vain to button his already buttoned fly, he was pouring out his fullness of soul to the shop's mongrel which had retreated to the back of its kennel. The pint-sized lover was made of sterner stuff and still retained some semblance of hope: he continued to fill pregnant Zoika's glass immoderately, persistently and humourlessly whining,

"Zoi, oi, Zoi, you aren't expecting a baby elephant are you?"

"Oh, go screw yerself..." was the semi-comatose Zoika's reply. But he badgered her so relentlessly with his question that Zoika was finally obliged to enquire what a baby elephant had to do with anything.

"Try feeling between my legs. I've got a baby elephant expecting down there," the little old man chortled at his joke, and for some reason shoved his own hand up Zoika's skirt. His grope brought him little joy: Zoika's frock, and the whole bench she was sitting on, were sopping wet.

"Zoika, you pissed yourself or what?" the reprobate enquired with sudden concern.

Zoika shook her head. She herself had little idea what was happening to her, but suddenly found this groping old man so disgusting that she violently swept her arm over the table, knocking all the glasses and bottles to the floor, and again shouting her rather limited: "Oh, go screw yerself..."

The crash of breaking glass instantly plucked Anna Ivanovna from her state of tender reverie. She was about to bark orders with her stentorian bass, but something in Zoika's expression held her back.

"Zoika, what is the matter?" the manageress enquired, with heavy emphasis on the "is".

"Pissed herself." The intrusive Romeo wrinkled his nose and pouted his lower lip in condolence.

"Shut your trap, you randy little runt." Anna Ivanovna came round the table, for some reason felt Zoika's head, whispered something in her ear, and started giving her large amounts of cold water to drink. But when it became clear that she was hurting below, and that the pain was not going away but, on the contrary, coming on more and more severely, Anna Ivanovna's remaining doubts were dispelled. "Some expert you are," she glowered at the groper. "Her waters've broken."

The party prepared to move.

2

The whole gathering went along with Zoika to the maternity hospital. It was not a long walk, four blocks or so, but the frost cleared their heads and it was only when they arrived at reception that the sugary, vinous heaviness returned. The mother-to-be was handed over to a cack-handed auxiliary nurse who swore like a trooper, and they all went on to Raissa's apartment to continue the party.

Zoika was definitely out of luck. The birth was difficult, with a breech presentation. Happily Professor Rakhlin from Leningrad was in Stargorod for the region's in-service training courses and was still in the maternity block at this late hour: he gave a masterful demonstration of Tsovianov's delivery technique.

Zoika, well under the influence from all the wine, reacted weakly to the pain. The truth of the matter was that she didn't care one way or the other: she didn't want this baby. She had miscarried her first. The second time she jumped, on Raissa's advice, from the roof of the shed flat on to her feet and practically finished herself off with the pain and the bleeding. She had only come to term this time through her own stupidity in having left it too late to get an abortion. She was pleased when she caught the end of the consultant's lecture to the effect that breech presentation babies were often stillborn or died within the first two or three days after birth; but when she heard the baby's cry she resigned herself. For some reason she had no doubt that this one was going to live.

And so it happened. The little blue baby born in the early hours of 14 January survived and was admitted to the congregation of the faithful on its fifth day in a biting Epiphany frost by Zoika's mother, who had insisted on observing this fundamental Orthodox rite. The boy was given the first name of Daniil in honour of his grandmother's father, and the patronymic, traditional for a fatherless child, of Ivanovich.

3

The childhood of Daniil Ivanovich was not without its difficulties. As far as eighteen-year-old Zoika was concerned, her little son was purely a drag on her riotous social life; so after her milk dried up, as it did catastrophically early, in the third month, after one of her drinking sprees, she became quite irresponsible about feeding him. She would sleep through the times for collecting his feeds, or drunkenly spill the precious milligrams over the table, or sometimes simply forget to shove the battered teat into his bawling mouth.

But, against the odds, the little lad grew bigger and got used to sucking his thumb in the absence of the teat, a bad habit he was to retain in later life. The voracious little mouth later twisted slightly downwards and to the right, distorted by his thumb; the little eyes, which at such a tender age should have been gazing at angels dancing above the cradle, had an alert gleam in them, and his little cauliflower ears even then picked up sounds from his surroundings with amazing sensitivity, prompting him to start yelling or lie still as the situation demanded. If mother came home drunk, for example, and not alone, the little person would first emit a desperate squeal to remind her of his existence but, detecting that nobody intended to take care of him for the time being, would fall silent and get to work on his thumb, or try to catch the chewed muslin sausage with a piece of bread in it and suck from it sour, life-giving juices detectable to him alone. Nevertheless, before going to bed his mother usually did stop his magpie-like maw with the calibrated baby's bottle, and he would get his feed for the night and quieten down or, tugging with his little fingers at his nappy, listen to the rustling sounds coming from the divan, and the amorous expletives of mother's latest transient beau. He was spared the usual penal Russian cocooning in swaddling clothes. His mother had heard somewhere that freer swaddling developed independence in a man, so bound him firmly and tightly but left his arms free.

Each morning, after milking the goat, at around ten o'clock, grandmother would appear, having made her way into town from the village on the other side of the lake. Hearing her heavy footfall in the hallway, the baby would start yelling heartrendingly in anticipation of the bottle of warm milk and his bath in the dented aluminium basin. Glistening afterwards from a liberal application of petroleum jelly, and wearing a clean nappy, he would fall asleep instantly, plunging head-long into that redemptive abyss in order to conserve his strength for the semi-starvation of the second half of the day when his grandmother, having cooed over him for as long as she dared, would disappear. She was afraid of her daughter, who was quite capable of setting about her when in a bad mood. Sighing heavily, and blaming only herself for an old fool stupid enough to produce such a monster, grandmother preferred to make herself scarce while the going was good.

But one day she left it too late. She had been tidying the house up, cooking the lunch, washing nappies, and had forgotten to keep an eye on the time. The boy, who was assertive and confident while grandmother was around, having peed himself, lost no time in drawing the world's attention to the fact. Grandmother melted instantly, and set her little angel down on the table to change him. A cold draught made him want to pee again and he spouted a little sparkling fountain in the air. His grandmother caught it in her hands and laughed, called it "dew from heaven; truly, dew from heaven!" and kissed her wet hands. She carried him back to the cot in order to replace the wet nappy on the table with another, clean one. At just that moment Zoika burst into the house like a she-wolf in a vicious temper, pushed her mother aside, and set to changing her son's nappy herself, lisping and shaking her head at him, already drunk. She was keen to demonstrate to the buoy-master cooling his heels in the hallway what a good and caring mother she was. At that point she had not yet lost hope of finding a permanent partner, and the buoy-master was tolerably young: under thirty, at least. Somehow she set about it wrong, and the baby was in any case all wet with dew from heaven. The thin little body slipped from her hands and smacked down on to the floor. The force of the fall was taken by his little bottom. The tiny legs knocked against the floor boards like two icicles, and Daniil squealed and struggled on the floor. All the blame, of course, was the old woman's for not having dried him, and not having looked after him properly, and, and, and...

No bones were broken, although the bruising on the injured buttocks did not go down for a week. Evidently, however, as his grandmother said, some artery had been nipped. His legs did not grow well after the accident. He was visibly short-legged in later life, and had the ambling gait of a cavalryman.

After that episode grandmother finally made her mind up, and when the opportunity presented itself, kidnapped her grandson and carried him off home to her village. He was out of Zoika's reach there: the village women would have stood up for the old woman; and, odd as it may seem, the intrepid Zoika had a great fear of ill repute. She was actually quite well pleased with the way things had turned out. She yelled and shrieked for the sake of decency, but then settled down to visiting on Sundays, and later stopped even that, dropping in only infrequently to "borrow" the odd ten or twenty roubles till pay-day.

Grandmother's cooking soon had the little boy recovering lost ground, but it was a long time before his face was free of scabbing; and his inclination to gluttony (which grandmother prided herself on) and his thumb sucking were to be with him for many years to come.

Even though he gorged himself on all that was put before him, and anything else he found around the place, at five he was still very small for his age, and quite abnormally taciturn. Other children his age were noticeably better built but, oddly enough, no sturdier. On his little duck legs he somehow managed to outrun them, climbing up on to sheds and the old boats at the lakeside, haring around on a rusty home-made cart, or playing in the dirt with the shaggy village dogs. For all that he showed no leadership potential in their gangs, and kept his head down. He seemed to be listening intently to something. His little body stretched out and became nimble, but because of his stunted legs (he had small feet and was forever wearing other children's cast-off shoes), he looked rather squat and his flat little face with its twisted mouth, bright little darting eyes, and cauliflower ears fitted his nickname to a tee. The other children called him Skunk.

He was the apple of grandmother's eye, and she was forever treating him to sweets and biscuits, pancakes and pies, but beyond that she largely left him to his own devices: she would either disappear to the vegetable plot or into the shed to look after her one and only nanny goat, or go off to forage in the food queues in town, or to stand through the services in church. Grandmother was devout. He grew up unconstrained, most of the time outside, and modelled himself more on his doggy friends than on grown-ups with whom, as yet, he had no dealings.

4

Grandmother would drag him along to church, sometimes on a Sunday, sometimes on a weekday, and outwardly he seemed to regard these visits much like their regular trips into town for groceries. In the big, redbrick church erected by some merchant it was invariably warm and dark, and while grandmother was doing her round, venerating and kissing the icons, he would hang around the candle counter where he contrived to receive an inordinate quantity of sweets, biscuits, and poppyseed-covered *baranka* bread rolls. Having performed her obeisances and bowed to each and everyone, grandmother would prise him out of the shop and take him over to the children's icons which depicted Artemy Verkolsky, slain by a thunderbolt, and Ioann and Yakov of Menyuzh. He could count on somebody nearby to re-tell him their stories, and knew by heart that the Blessed Artemy "was filled with dread at the wondrous manifestation of God's power and, afeared of the great thunder and the bright lightning, surrendered up his spirit"; and that the five-year-old Yakov of Menyuzh, while playing tip-cat, accidentally struck his brother with the bat and killed him and then, fearful of his mother's wrath, hid in the stove where he suffocated in the smoke. Little Daniil listened to the old ladies, his eyes darting impatiently hither and thither, seeking a quiet corner where he could hide away and scoff the presents received at the candle counter in peace. They misread his unvarying alertness and total lack of interest in the stories as the paying of close attention. The women talked on and on about the "little children" while he, after giving the icons a perfunctory peck in their lower corner, would make himself scarce and, with his eyes gleaming out of the semi-darkness of a side chapel, would silently study this curious collection of human beings. Tucked away as inconspicuously as a frog under a log, he took in the booming of the deacon and the flowing of the liturgy. His fresh young mind readily memorized the Church Slavonic of the service, without making the slightest attempt to understand the meaning of the archaic words.

When grandmother took him up to the priest for confession, he stood there obediently, obediently placed his head under the penitential stole, and obediently then proceeded to communion, unfalteringly going through the requisite ritual. Grandmother's old lady friends stroked his hair, touched by his piety, and brought him mugs of watered down communion wine, and mistook his amazing stamina for a degree of humility rarely to be found in young children.

At the end of the service, after kissing the Cross, many of the congregation went out, through the church railings, and down to the river bank. The church was built, as is common enough, on a prominent windswept mound where, according to legend, the town had had its beginnings. This whole district with its timber market, its fish wharf, its factory workshops, and its prerevolutionary official institutions and government offices, now divided up into peculiarly shaped communal apartments, was called the Mound, or Slav Mound, or Slavno, and in all Stargorod there were no street gangs more truculent and fearsome than the young denizens of the mean streets of this crowded working class district, who were collectively known as the Slavno Kids, or simply the Slavs.

The hill commanded a panoramic view of the town, the kremlin with its pocked walls, the proud monasteries upstream and downstream, custodians and owners in times long past of the rights of ingress and egress by river. These were now the premises of Technical College No. 6 and the local polytechnic institute.

On the hill itself had stood a monastery founded by St Andronicus "the Roman". The ancient monastic cells had not survived, and in the nineteenth century the city Duma had erected on the sacred site a massive five-domed redbrick edifice which had come through the postrevolutionary upheavals unscathed and was the only one of the churches of Stargorod to have maintained uninterrupted its tradition of Christian witness. On the river bank below the church, on a scrap of land not eroded by the water, lay the sacred rock. It was a large, smooth boulder, blue-green in colour and with light sparkling in it here and there. It clearly was not of these parts, resembling neither the porous local red sandstone on which the local churches and kremlin towers were built, nor the morainic boulders from the fields which provided solid foundations, heating stones for bathhouses, and the paving for the old roads.

The rock was alien, miraculous and sacred. According to legend Andronicus sailed on it from Rome itself, standing aloft

15

"as on a raft of timbers". What was more, it lay on the bank just above the water level, there "where first it struck the land", and neither moss nor the green fronds of mermaid's hair would grow on it. It had not bedded into the earth, but seemed to rest firm and fast upon its surface.

It was to this rock that the old ladies customarily processed at the end of the service. They descended the steep, muddy steps, holding on to a handrail and taking a rest now and again on the benches placed at intervals on the descent. Under Bolshevik rule the rock did not qualify for a metal surround, but candles had always been implanted in the soft earth and lit in defiance of all prohibition; at Easter painted eggs were left there, and rice and millet were scattered in the form of a cross, to be eaten by the town's sparrow population.

Crossing herself, grandmother got down on her knees, kissed the rock, and had little Daniil repeat the ritual after her. The old ladies would then recall piecemeal words from the legend: "So then St Andronicus saw the wickedness of the ways of Rome and sailed miraculously to our land of Orthodoxy". "True words, my dear. Where else will you find such beauty as in Russia? I was standing in the church yesterday, and the Holy Father's words, you must believe me, burned their way straight into my heart. How I wept, sinful old fool that I am. I stood there, and the tears fairly poured down my cheeks; I felt so pure, so pure in my soul..."

"Yes, he is a good man, the Father."

Little Daniil stood silently, looking down into the flowing river (you were supposed to approach the rock this way, facing towards the east) and heard not one word of what they were saying. Around the rock there spread the sweetish, pungent smell of new mown hay, while from the water rose the cool vapours of the river. His gaze, directed downwards with slightly downcast eyes, his intense, severe, unspeaking demeanour, the expression of an inner strength which had been with him since birth, touched all who saw him and rewarded his grand-mother a hundredfold.

He really did have an inner strength beyond his years. He never cried, no matter how he hurt himself. He rarely fought with other boys, enduring any insult or childish rudeness; but he did not run away when he was abused, merely stood stock still, looking morosely down at the ground. Only one time, when one of them slighted his mother, he hurled himself at a well-built six-year-old, leaped up on to his back, and clamped his teeth on the nape of his neck. They were separated by grown-ups, but he was known thereafter as "the mad dog", and considered somebody whom it was best not to taunt.

When he was five and a half, one July, he played outside until late and, when he got hungry, came home. Grandmother was lying on the kitchen floor with her legs twisted at an unnatural angle. The corner of the kitchen table, grandmother's temple, and the linoleum around her head were covered in congealed blood. There was a rag on the floor and a pail of water: grandmother had been washing the floor when she slipped and hit the side of her head on the sharp corner. The head was now thrown backwards, her unblinking stare directed upwards to where the wallpaper was coming unstuck.

He walked round the body, touched a cold finger nail, pressed her cheek with his finger, froze into immobility for a moment, sniffing her, but there was no smell at all. He listened intently and, detecting no sound of breathing, stepped over her head, took from the table a hunk of bread and the quart can with the evening's milk from the goat, and climbed up on to the divan. He ate the bread and drank the milk. Then he started looking at the body. In silence he studied the face, hands, the dirty bare legs, the cracked, grimy feet. Then he switched his attention to the wall, and the same piece of wall-paper which the old lady was staring at with her glassy eyes. He sat, not turning off the light, not moving, until morning.

As it grew dark the hundred watt bulb in the kitchen seemed

to burn more brightly, flooding everything with warmth and unwavering light. He did not feel any draught, and ceased to make out the pattern of the wallpaper. Like a blind person he sensed the distant presence of objects only through the skin on his face. The closed door cut off the rest of the house, but at the same time gave peace, and the dead body was as natural as a stool, or the iron on the stove which had grown cold.

This was how he was found by a neighbour who bought milk each morning from grandmother. He was sitting on the little kitchen divan next to the rigid old woman, huddled up but seemingly unafraid, and as always, sucking his thumb. His eyes were watering and swollen from the sleepless night, but had lost nothing of their gleam. The neighbour came in, stepping quietly on the rag mats. The little boy probably did not hear her footsteps, but evidently detected the air moving as she approached and, like a little animal, started in surprise and even blushed slightly. Sensing through the trembling fingers which touched his hair and face the depth of the speech-less woman's horror, he just turned his face slightly towards her and said, "My gran is dead", took his thumb out of his mouth, flopped back on the divan and fell sound asleep.

The village people remembered this as they muttered at Zoika's selling the house for next to nothing. Little Daniil was untroubled by their concern, and went back to live in the town.

5

Zoika didn't manage to get him into a nursery school, so he was dragged along to his mother's workplace. There he had total freedom to play in the store room, or run all over the warehouse where he was allowed to eat any fruit he fancied, but most of the time he ran around in the waste land behind the shop. As before he got on better with animals than with

18

other children. He made friends with the dogs, and could watch their extravagant marriages for hours on end. The sight of dogs mating aroused an already awakening interest in his own body. He would follow the dogs for miles, but had some special sense which enabled him to find his way back to the shop. He observed a cat playing with a half-dead sparrow, and watched closely how a many-hued dragonfly, covered in voracious ants, writhed dying from their poison. He experienced no sadistic arousal from all this: he was simply studying the ins and outs of life and death. He chased the pigeons and crows on the rubbish tips. Small boys from the houses round about were strictly forbidden to have anything to do with him. He possessed an intricate repertoir of swear words (which they were supposed not to know). With his gammy legs and ragged appearance he was viewed with apprehension by respectable parents. At the sight of him, the small boys would shout, "Twisty mouth Skunky, twisty mouth Skunky!" and he gave up seeking their company.

He made up a game for himself which consisted of setting one tin can on top of another, walking back, and throwing stones at them, trying to knock off the top one or the bottom one, depending on the task he had set himself. It wasn't long before he scored a hit every time: he had a keen eye.

This game spawned a more serious entertainment. Hiding in the store room, he waged war on the rats. He had a way of sitting motionless, waiting for the stupid animals to creep out of their holes. You had to not look at them directly: he had learned from grandmother's nanny goat how to locate things by hearing. Slightly moving his head with his sensitive cauliflower ears, he would sit clutching a heavy ballbearing in his fist. He seemed to be sleeping with his eyes barely open, but when a rat ran out into the light, he would suddenly hurl the ballbearing at it. He rarely missed, but in order to stun it you had to hit it right in the eye, and then finish it off with a stick. Most often the rat would leap in the air with a disgusting squeak and disappear back into its hole in the wall or among the sacks of vegetables. Twice, though, he managed to kill fat rats with long, hairless tails which looked as if they belonged on a beetroot. He was very proud of this.

The women in the shop soon stopped noticing him. He showed no reaction to their passing pats and cuddles and tried to keep out of their sight, which naturally offended them. Anna Ivanovna, marching from the store room to the shop, would see the little figure huddled in some corner and, returning to the counter, always shouted over to Zoika, "That little bollockbrain of yours is still hunting rats."

"Oh, screw him. At least he's not under my feet," Zoika would respond dismissively.

He really did look as though he had a screw loose, always tatty from his wanderings through waste land and rubbish dumps, wearing a scruffy coat or a torn sweater, little rubber boots and a hat of some unimaginable style, or with his long unwashed pallid head bare, revealing the sparse hair popularly considered a sign of inebriacy, or at least of a brooding and anaemic disposition. He ate when the chance offered itself, devouring every last scrap, then fell back from the emptily gleaming plate and lay inert for a time while the food settled in his bulging stomach. Then he would leave the table and be ready for more excursions and hunting; or he would settle down quietly somewhere on a sofa or in an armchair, staring at the television and sucking his beloved thumb.

His mother's male visitors mostly treated him like an inanimate object. Few tried to gain his goodwill, and any who did received a chill blast of loathing for their pains.

The only exception was Uncle Kolya, who drove a big, heavy timber truck and tarried in Zoika's apartments longer than the rest. Uncle Kolya, to be sure, was also fond of the drink, especially after a heavy day; but little Daniil immediately sensed that drink did not have the same hold over him as over the others. Even after a bottle of vodka he did not turn

20

into a brainless, snoring monster, did not hiccough, did not belch in the lavatory, fart uninhibitedly, yell the house down, break the dishes or beat his mother. Uncle Kolya washed his clothes himself, took him and his mother to the cinema to see a French film with Jean-Paul Belmondo, and sometimes collected them from the vegetable shop in his huge truck with its clattering iron trailer. He even let Daniil sit at the steering wheel.

While Uncle Kolya was around his mother tidied herself up, began putting on lipstick, and sometimes dabbed behind her ears and under her armpits from a little bottle of Red Moscow perfume. It smelled unbearably yummy.

Uncle Kolya brought them game from the forest. He had a single-barrelled shotgun, and if he did not bag something himself on the way back, other hunters and lumberjacks whom he knew would share with him. He brought mainly deciduous forest game: black-cock, wood and hazel grouse. A whole pile of tasty little hazel grouse which he would bake in the oven in foil. He and Daniil plucked them together, because his mother did not like to.

One time he took the boy out to work with him. It was already almost evening when they reached the felling zone, loaded the trailer with sticky pine trunks, and spent the night in a forest hut with the lumberjacks. The best thing was on the way back. One of the men took a lift with them back into town. Uncle Kolya got him to drive, put a handful of cartridges into his jacket pocket, tethered himself to the door handle by his broad officer's belt, and stood outside on the running board with his shotgun. The truck moved along slowly, barely crawling, with the engine running evenly, no backfiring.

"The main thing is, you have to keep the sound steady, otherwise they take fright and fly away," the man explained.

"They" were the wood grouse sitting right up in the tops of the pine trees, large, bluish black, stretching out their long necks to follow the progress of this strange rumbling creature.

"It's people they fear, not trucks," the man went on to

explain. On the running board Uncle Kolya pressed himself against the truck, pointing his gun forwards. Soon he fired. A large cock bird was dislodged from its bough and flew straight upwards before beginning suddenly to fall, somersaulting in the air and crashing down heavily on the road. Uncle Kolya shot almost a dozen of them that time. He gave several to his travelling companion, and the remainder to Zoika's friends, Anna Ivanovna and Raissa. Even the neighbour across the landing got a plump wood grouse. On the doorpost above the entrance to their flat he nailed the tail of a cock hazel grouse spread out like a fan. It hung there for many years, even after Uncle Kolya was gone. Having had one too many, Uncle Kolya drove his truck one winter into one of the swamps which did not freeze and sank with it. It was the devil of a job dragging the loaded truck back out, even using a heavy tractor.

Daniil remembered that trip to the forest. Sitting all alone at home waiting for his mother to come back, he re-lived the sounds of the hunt: a love of the chase had been born in him. The memories gave him physical pleasure. Closing his eyes, he wriggled in the armchair, sucking his thumb manically. The winter Uncle Kolya died he had already started school.

6

Skunk did not excel at school. He learned to add and subtract, divide and multiply, to trace the letters of the alphabet, and read just about passably, with a certain amount of exasperated prompting. And that was it. Every class in the school had three or four of these sad little proletarians from the Slavno area, but the teachers accepted the challenge and did their best to get them into technical college.

Memorizing even a short poem by Pushkin or Lermontov was quite beyond Skunk, and yet he had an exceptional tactile, visual and aural memory. He seemed to divine his way to school using all his senses, registering barely perceptible inclines and declines, faults in the road and twists of the pavement like a blind person. A rustle, a noise, a whisper in class, the twittering of the birds outside the window heard or overheard today or yesterday or the day before lodged in his memory like so many musical phrases and came back to him unbidden during lessons. Then he would switch off and turn into a plaster cast of the ideal pupil sitting with back straight and arms folded on the desk, his shining eyes looking straight through the wall at nothing.

He was quite without fear of the dark. The changing rooms of the school gymnasium were in a basement, and intended to double as an air-raid shelter in the event of war. Once when somebody turned the lights out a panic-stricken stampede ensued, and it was Skunk who found the way out for his class-mates who were bumping into walls and blundering about in corners. Complementing this physical, tactile memory was an uncanny sense of direction. He was in his element in the wilds, in the woods on one of the class's periodical Sunday trips. Nobody beat Skunk at mushroom picking.

He didn't flaunt these unusual talents, and indeed went to considerable lengths to hide them. At school he was the inconspicuous little grey mouse: not led, but not a leader; not an outsider, but his own man.

Skunk paid a price for his independence. He was never seen at birthday parties, and never invited anyone home. The sour smell of his mother's lair on the ground floor did not favour having friends round to play. He wandered around the city, and people knew his face in the factory workshops or down at the fish wharf, but that was as far as it went. He made no friends, and in summer caught fish on his own, boiling them up into soup in a billy-can, with a jar of spices and a spoon nicked from someone's boat.

In bushes down by the river he built a lean-to shelter, furnished it with old quilted jackets and soft rags, and would

23

sleep there, setting off at dawn to fish. His mother wasn't bothered. She knew he would be home when he got hungry. At night he would go down to St Andronicus's rock to gather up the candle ends, and his lean-to always smelled invitingly of warm wax.

The rock figured in one of his secrets, perhaps indeed his biggest secret. He had come down one night as usual, picked up the candle ends and pushed them into his anorak pockets, when he suddenly sensed, and only then actually saw, that the rock was not lying as it should have been on the ground, but was hovering just above it. There was a gap beneath it he could have slipped his hand into, if he hadn't been afraid of getting it crushed. The night was clear, with a full moon high in the sky; there was a profound stillness, with not a soul to be seen. He felt the rock all over. His fingers slid easily over a pleasantly smooth surface, detecting nothing out of the ordinary. Then, without a moment's hesitation, he clambered up on to the rock, settled himself comfortably in the middle in his favourite slightly hunched position, sucking his thumb in the confident expectation that something extraordinary was going to happen, and stayed perfectly still, taking in the silence. Soon he felt an inexplicable lightness with the whole of his being. The rock swayed slightly in the night air. He felt neither hot nor cold, but only very much at peace. The river was flowing underneath his feet, and time seemed somehow altered. No more than a moment passed, and yet when the rock settled once more in its place it was already growing light.

He climbed off and bent down to check, but the rock was resting firmly on the ground. A few sparks glittered in its blue-green depths. Daniil knew for a fact that the rock had hovered with him on it above the river bank during the night, but he also knew that if he mentioned it to anyone they would think he was crazy.

7

He had another secret. Although he didn't appear fickle about his food, and at home ate whatever there was, however and whenever it appeared, in fact he thought obsessively about fancy food far beyond their means. He was possessed by the idea of it, engulfed and enslaved by gastronomic yearnings. It was not so much hunger as a burning envy which troubled his flesh no less than the shameful dreams which now disturbed him.

The allure of attributes specific to the opposite sex, unattainable but longed for, tormented him, and the rapture, the fantasies and, accompanying them, the bizarre promptings of his flesh like some dirty, cloying disease, set his heart pounding. There was something genuinely mad about the way colours would well up out of his memory, smells, tastes, all in a complete jumble: femininity and purity; smuttiness and the half covert glance of some self-possessed girl from one of the senior classes on the dance floor; a sudden wild, empty-headed guffaw; the dizzying smell of ammonia emanating from the junior girls' lavatory on the first floor; the final, spiritual look on the face of his dead grandmother; the perfect, frenzied beauty of girl athletes running towards the finishing line in the school sports stadium; and images which invaded his mind without rhyme or reason: the sharp blade of a knife running up and down a leather strap; the taut white water rapids in the river; the proud turning towards the sun of a moist tulip bud; the snail-like labyrinth of a textbook diagram of the ear, with arrows running all over it to indicate the path followed by sounds; and the smell of singed feathers, of a daisy in the meadow, of wet dog fur; and many other things, many, many more.

There was only one defence against these obsessions. He would bury his face in the pillow and shut his eyes tight until fiery circles appeared and blotted everything out. He would block his ears with his fingers and thus, immersed in complete darkness and a lifeless hush, rolled up in a ball under the blanket, he would fight off impudent, throbbing temptation.

No doubt it was all to do with his mother. Just as he could not bear the smell of alcohol, which was with him always and everywhere in his drink-sodden home, so neither could he bring himself to look at the tackle sprouting below his belly. He was afraid of it. He knew perfectly well what his mother and her gentlemen visitors got up to behind the flimsy curtain. For some reason she loved them all dearly and took good care of them, even the ones who were filthy, or pissed out of their minds; the ones who whined and those who used her shamelessly for the sole purpose of getting drunk out of their skulls and jumping naked into her bed. For some reason none of them stayed around long, except for Uncle Kolya that time. They came and went, and left their slivers of used soap behind in the bathroom, and thought nothing of washing or shaving with someone else's leftover soap or scraping their bristles with another man's razor blade. He grew up among them, seemingly paying no notice, but he could not and did not accept them.

He discovered a risky new game: picking pockets; and the clients he favoured were his mother's old flames. Not that they had much in their pockets at the best of times, but what little there was he filched adroitly. He would come upon them all over town: at beer stalls; queueing for vodka; at the bazaar; sometimes out taking the air with a whole family of kids and their lawful wedded wife in tow. He would target his victim, play him like a fish, sometimes all the way to the man's home; sometimes, indeed, he would stalk them for days on end, studying their habits, until the right moment arrived, in a jostling crowd or a queue or a packed bus on the way home from their shift at work, or on pay day when his client was drunk. He could steal from them without even looking, facing away from the victim or "old goat", as he called them to himself, adopting the most offensive term from their own sleazy vocabulary.

Most of them were ex-cons, or at least of that ilk: sloggers, sad cases from the lower strata of the unskilled workforce, dull-eyed men defeated by life whose two remaining ambitions were to hit the bottle and have their end away. For some reason this had to be with his mother or others like her: cowed, uncomplaining women, waiting for the next slave-driver to come along as if he were God's gift.

Skunk ripped them off and then, with any luck, he would even get to watch the pathetic slobs yelling and cursing and grinding their nicotine-stained teeth, deprived of their one hope of redemption: to buy ever more vodka, wine and beer. He chuckled, inwardly gloating, his face as always inscrutable. He exulted in their wretchedness, imagining the slanging match when they got home, the shrieking wife depending on a pay packet she would not now be seeing. He knew well enough that some such incident could lead to real violence, to the casualty ward, sometimes even to the cemetery; and of course to prison, back to prison, their home from home, where they really all belonged anyway.

Afterwards he would run to a food shop and buy himself a mountainous pile of cakes and sweets and fruit juice. With his own money. He could buy a chicken. Two, if he felt like it. And butter, the ordinary kind and the chocolate flavoured. And a proper cake, "Morning Dew", or "Napoleon", or "Nut Crumb", whichever. He did all this shopping at the far end of the town, well away from Slavno where he might be recognized. He had it all worked out. He made his way home on foot, always, with a rucksack specially acquired to hide his goodies in. He would go back to his lean-to, or hide away in the basement of a disused pumping station, depending on the weather and time of year. If it was warm he would light a campfire on the river bank; if it was raining, or in the winter, he would fire up an old Dutch stove in his basement which was still in working order, and brew up tea and roast his chickens over the embers on a special contraption he had made out of heavy gauge wire. And if there was any money left over, he would hide that here too, in a secret place.

He went hunting again only when his supplies had run out. He never bought goods, only food he liked and which he could enjoy in a single meal, leaving no evidence. But he could stalk his victim for a long time, letting him graze; the heat of the chase, even the let-down when he missed a trick, gave him a purely animal pleasure.

Oddly enough, he had only to start hunting a new quarry for his troublesome dreams to vanish. He would fall immediately into a deep, contented sleep, just as he had as a child after his bath in the battered aluminium tub. His lips glistened from the rich, nutritious food, his stomach rumbled pleasurably, and the cream filling of the cakes, the stuffed roast chicken or pork kebabs roasted on the embers brought an expression of bliss to his face. The slight twist of his lips straightened, and the suggestion of a glow, the semblance of a smile, only it certainly was not a smile, emanated from his flat little face as it relaxed.

8

In the eighth grade Zhenka was put to sit next to him, evidently on the principle that it was best to put the rotten apples in the same barrel, pairing one no-hoper with another. She made no attempt to learn anything, just goggled at the blackboard with her big warm eyes and flapped her fan-like eyelashes at the rest of the class, and the schoolmistress had evidently resigned herself to settling for that. Zhenka, like Skunk, was one of the Slavno set. Her little black apron was always clean and well-ironed, and she herself was sweetly aromatic thanks to a wooden phial of Bulgarian rose oil which nestled permanently in her little pocket. Her mother was a dressmaker.

Carefree and languid, rosy cheeked and healthy, solidly put together but by no means fat, Zhenka would have been the ideal model for a poster of a peasant girl overfulfilling the five-year plan. Or at least, she would have been but for her phlegmatic air of worldly weariness. If Zhenka was required to sit at her desk, she would; and if she had been required to go hoe beetroot, she would doubtless have gone without bothering her pretty head about it in the slightest.

Moose's lot, probably the hardest of the Slavno gangs from Technical College No. 6, were always waiting for Zhenka as she left school. She would walk off briskly with them, their arms around her, she carrying her little briefcase, and everybody knew that if they laid a finger on her they could expect to be slashed. The lads had razors and flick knives, and flaunted them.

Zhenka liked chomping apples and it was here that Skunk and she found common ground. He would bring apples from the shop where his mother worked, and she would chomp them. That was the word she used herself: "Think I fancy a chomp...," she would say, and Skunk would look on. She had really good teeth, white and even and strong.

He fed her apples for the whole of the first half-semester: Zhenka rewarded him by saying which cinema they took her to; how much money Moose had (a lot); who Moose had just done over or who he was just about to. (Relations between the different Slavno gangs were strained and often erupted into pitched battles.) Skunk was all ears. Moose's gang was of interest to him, to tell the truth, only to the extent that it exercised property rights over Zhenka, but his hopes of hearing anything about that side of things were disappointed. Zhenka knew the rules.

Skunk eyed her with such undisguised enthusiasm that even the impenetrably placid Zhenka could not overlook it.

"What you gawping at. Fancy me, or what?"

"Yes," he said openly and unafraid.

"It's nice you fancy me. Lots of people do." The bland indifference of her tone instantly cooled his ardour.

Imperceptibly, very slowly, some time towards spring, when even Skunk's stoicism was beginning to buckle, Zhenka began to melt. She would ask him questions just a little too often; sit rather too near him, moving their chairs together until they touched; and he was granted permission (he could tell one day that it was okay) to put his hand just above her plump little knee.

After that he asked her out to the cinema, operating to a plan, but Zhenka said no.

"Pack it in. You'd never get away with it," she said, but whether condoling or simply informing him of the situation he had no way of telling. She placed his hand consolingly on her knee. "Only while we're at school, okay? They'd kill you. You don't know what they're like."

She resolved the problem straightforwardly and without regret. Skunk did not remove his hand. He had no intention of falling out with her, but neither had he any intention of quitting. He needed a different approach. What it might be he did not yet know.

9

Intuition, a supreme animal intuition above words or logic, suggested the answer: he would stalk his rival, find out who it was he had to fight. Moose arrived at the school flanked by two lieutenants, Budgie and Dove. They shouted a lot, and flapped and capered, their mayhem, which could be dangerous for those who got too near, providing a foil for their deliberate, slow-moving, sleepy-eyed leader. Dove and Budgie took "loans" from the pupils, flashing a blade here, edgily snapping a flick-knife open there. Moose, needless to say, did not demean himself with such matters, but sat in the little square beside the children's swings, his hair gleaming as black as his winkle-picker shoes with their angled heels, smoking a chic Bulgarian *papirosa* cigarette from a red pack. It was long and slender and had a gold mouthpiece, and he never passed it over for someone else to finish or take a drag. Instead he would look up silently and appraisingly at the supplicant, silently slip his hand inside his jacket, produce the whole pack, flip it open with the top pointing away from himself, and click his lighter. Letting someone else light up from your own cigarette was uncool, little better than kissing a man, "rooster petting", the ultimate offence in the breezy world of tomorrow's jailbirds.

Zhenka always went to him with her head bowed submissively. She would nod in greeting, ignoring the antics of Budgie and Dove. They might pinch her bottom, or even slip a hand up under her apron, but she had first to meet his gaze, and only after that would the boss rise from his bench, put an arm round her, and move off. Sometimes a whole horde would meet up together, including other girls, but Moose always remained seated, spitting on the ground in a special way, his authority unquestionable and final.

Moose radiated power. Skunk could feel it even watching from his hiding place behind a garage. He felt drawn irresistibly to the bench beside the swings, he would have given his right arm just to sit there unspeaking, accepted, next to brooding Moose. But the aberration was dispelled the instant he remembered Zhenka whispering, "Pack it in. You don't know what they're like..."

They did not conceal their movements. It was a simple matter to follow them. They walked steadily in one direction, sometimes taking up the whole of the pavement, past the transport depot of the agricultural fertilizer factory, past the fish wharf, the factory workshops, the disused pumping station (his pumping station), across wasteland (a football field) to a large, recently built nine-storey apartment block now occupied by the city's top officials. Skunk knew for a fact that not one of them was officially registered as living there. He spent many hours circling the apartment block, peering up at the windows. People would drift lazily out of its depths, throw open a quarter-light for ventilation, close or open curtains, water house plants, but no member of Moose's gang ever appeared. He cased the stairwell. The basement and attic were padlocked. There was no way the basement door could be locked from inside; the attic, however, was secured by a grille which also cut off half a flight of stairs and could easily be locked from the other side by pushing a hand between the bars. They had to be in the attic.

In an adjacent identical apartment block he had no trouble sawing through the hasp of the padlock on the grille to the attic and going up. But the attic was empty, except for pigeon droppings. A breeze blew from ventilation ducts. The only place they could be using was a room housing the elevator in the middle. This too was padlocked, but he sawed through that also and found himself in a ready made den. In the centre were winches serving two liftshafts; on two of the walls there were large insulated central heating pipes at waist level. Stale air, cement dust, a strong smell of industrial grease, a bare light bulb suspended from the ceiling. In the far corner a door led out on to the roof. The unpredictable cutting in of the lift machinery was a drawback, and the vibrating floor, but you could get used to that.

He stepped out on to the soft tarred roof. On the neighbouring apartment block, a lone figure among the TV aerials, stood Moose looking down on the city.

The stocky figure, his sloping, hunched shoulders, his close-fitting buttoned-up dark grey jacket, the hands held rigidly by his sides, was outlined against a washed out sky with clouds which seemed to have been feathered in with a fine paintbrush. Leaning against a wall, Skunk reacted physically to this mute statue mounted in the bricks between two quivering television aerials. There was a smell of rusty metal and wet tarmac. No trace now of the swaggering dandy: all that had been left behind in the little square. Only a deflated, intense brooding. Far below the greens and browns of the city were spread before him, diminutive and insubstantial.

So now he knew the whereabouts of Moose's lair. It remained to pay him a visit. He took in the situation for a week and then, one morning when he could count on finding the elevator room unoccupied, skipped school and made his move. The grille was fastened with a simple lock which he picked in an instant with a nail. The elevator room boasted a table, chairs, and a torn leather armchair, evidently the potentate's throne. On the floor lay a striped mattress from which a sour smell proceeded.

There was no problem about hiding. The builders had used the attic to dump planks, paint crates, two large containers of dried-up whitewash, trestles spattered with paint, and a heap of petrified sacks of cement. Where once the door had had a mortice lock, it now had only a gaping hole, a perfect peephole. In an emergency he could vanish simply by slipping round behind the room.

Which he duly did. Skunk had little more than an hour to wait, sitting behind the cans of whitewash while the extortionists were exacting tribute and making their way unhurriedly back to base. They went in, closing the door behind them, the three of them and Zhenka. Skunk contained his impatience for a further ten minutes before creeping up to the peephole. Sprawled around the table, they were swigging bad port accompanied by curd cheese *syrki* and bread. Half way through the second bottle Moose prodded Zhenka in the back. "Let's have it, then!" he commanded phlegmatically, as in all probability he had a hundred times before. Zhenka rose obediently. Budgie and Dove jumped up and took her matter-of-factly over to the armchair.

While they were at it, doggy fashion, like fitful little steam engines, Moose lit up a long *Femina* cigarette and averted his gaze disdainfully. Surprisingly, though, even when he went to work, holding a new cigarette away from himself in a lordly manner, Zhenka's expression remained blank. She stared with her great calf-like eyes at the wall much as she stared at the blackboard at school, as if just about to say, "Sku-unk, think I fancy a chomp."

Skunk declined to watch them finishing the wine and playing cards (Dove was already shuffling the pack for Moose). Everything was clearly being done in accordance with some unchallengeable ritual. He stole away from the door and went down to the street. He knew what he was going to do. He had only to think of Zhenka and her waifish clothing; to see her brushing imaginary dust specks off the little apron and straightening the pleats of her dress before sitting down at the table again and taking up her tumbler of wine, but sitting now over to one side in order not to be in the way of the card players. For some reason, though, he could not stop thinking about Moose: Moose, brooding, standing in isolation on the roof gazing down on the city; Moose as he had seen him the week before, not as he had seen him today, thrusting galvanically like a clown, to the accompaniment of rumbling elevator machinery, into a totally turned off Zhenka.

10

Curiously enough, now that he was fired by an idea and again pursuing a definite purpose, circling in on his quarry, he lost all interest in the primary cause. He moved his chair in the classroom over to the window and, to Zhenka's astonished enquiry, "Sku-unk, wotcha doing?", replied unambiguously, "Nothing. Wotcha mooing?"

After that they didn't speak or even look at each other again. Zhenka decamped across the gangway shortly afterwards to the back row of desks and seated herself next to a great lumbering, pimply oaf whose one topic of conversation was the motorbike waiting patiently for him in the country, and what a great time he was going to have bombing about on it all summer. Skunk did not even look in their direction, having other things to think about.

He was reborn now as Moose's shadow, often skipping lessons to stalk and prowl. He would lurk for hours near the apartment block, waiting for them to come back out into the open to see Zhenka home before wandering off themselves or, more interestingly, going out on business. They were sneak thieves, whence the money, ripping off anything that was lying about unattended and fencing it to an Azerbaidzhani shoeshine at the railway station. In March they did over the store at the transport depot, making off with small, heavy objects in holdalls and rucksacks. Budgie and Dove used a gun to blast a battered outboard motor off a boat, and Skunk heard Moose promising to nail their balls to the wall, just in case they were in danger of forgetting who was boss. Come April they turned over the sports store, aided and abetted this time by two accomplices. Moose directed operations from outside, and it was he who found a home for the loot, and distributed the rewards. Skunk was there once to observe the dividing of the spoils, Moose pulling a wallet from his breast pocket, peeling notes off a wad with a spit-dampened finger, and shoving them into Dove's pants and inside Budgie's shirt.

Skunk was everywhere now: lurking in gateways and stairwells, in squares, on park benches, behind advertising pillars, in bushes, derelict sheds and garages, in the cabs and backs of trucks, at slippery roadsides: anywhere he could see without being seen (and not infrequently even hear), and where he could store everything away in his mind. Picking pockets went by the board: he simply didn't have time. Sometimes he didn't have time even to eat, but this was no great hardship for him. He could go without food for days and then, like a wolf, make up for it in one go, gorging himself to the point of hiccups before lapsing into a blissful torpor.

His moment finally came. At the end of April Zhenka fell

sick and stopped coming to school. Moose and his merry men continued raking in the danegeld when school was over, and Skunk continued his vigil sitting on a rusty bucket behind the garages. Until one day they split up. Dove and Budgie were given their orders and, nodding assent, headed off away from the den. Moose sat where he was a while longer for appearances' sake, but then he too got to his feet.

Dove and Budgie had possibly been detailed to go to the wine shop, or perhaps somewhere else. That didn't matter. What did matter was that Moose was going to the apartment block on his own. Skunk gave him three or four minutes before himself scurrying in the entrance. He followed him up and into the attic, his nostrils scenting some special vibrancy in the air. The cement dust was shaking on one of the elevator winches as it operated. Skunk sidled over to the door out on to the roof. Just like that other time Moose was standing near the edge, his back towards Skunk, smoking. Asking for it.

Coolly, practised (how many times he had rehearsed this in his mind), Skunk placed a trainer on the dull bitumen. Three steps and then one almighy shove right in Moose's back. Throwing out his arms, Moose performed a swallow dive, screaming only at the very last moment. Skunk was already hurrying towards the stairwell landing. He snapped the lock to and polished it with his sleeve (knowing all about fingerprints). Two minutes later he was downstairs. He walked coolly out of the entrance, turned coolly into the sidestreet, stood half an hour or so behind a wall in the little courtyard of the work-shops, on a rubbish tip behind the rusting skeleton of a truck. He killed time, watered the flat tyre on one of the wheels with an unsteady jet, and rubbed his dry but suddenly itchy eyes. Then, making a detour and coming back from the opposite direction through the vegetable plots, he went to take a look.

Moose had fallen in front of the apartment block, right in the middle of a wet, muddy flowerbed which, this early in the spring, had yet to be dug over, among the battered and broken, whitish stems of last year's flowers. Skunk did not go too near, firmly gripping the branch of an apple tree which screened him. He coldbloodedly observed the apartment-dwellers, the police, the ambulancemen, and Dove and Budgie, crestfallen, scared, their overwrought bravado quelled. Strangely, when Moose was being moved on to a stretcher, it seemed to Skunk that the powerful, muscular body was not rigid in death like his grandmother's, but sagging like a jelly, all the willpower gone out of it. He seemed to be being rolled over the ground on to the waiting canvas.

Dove and Budgie received different treatment. He spotted them the very next day at the railway station queueing for pies. Skunk helped a citizen in front of them in the queue out of his bulging wallet and redistributed the contents: the man's papers he slipped to Dove, and the money and wallet went to Budgie. The rest was simplicity itself: passengers were constantly pushing their way through the queue. There was wheezing and foot shuffling, muttering and arm waving and swearing as suitcases were squeezed through. In the chaos of the train station nobody was thinking; everybody was in a rush to get somewhere, or queueing for something, or waiting for someone. It was the perfect setting for his chosen revenge. Dove and Budgie were pressing against the robbed citizen, impelled by a well dressed fat woman with two small children. She in turn was being pushed forward by a soldier and a Georgian with a sack and, to crown it all, someone was shrieking in front at the counter in a grating, reedy voice over something they thought had not been divided properly. Stage One, he lifted the wallet. Stages Two and Three, he fitted up Dove and Budgie. Stage Four, having waited until there were only five or six people left in front, shielding himself behind a porter, Skunk moved in on the citizen, shoved his hand in the man's pocket with contrived clumsiness, whipped it back out, and vanished. An irate yell duly followed, the police were called, and Dove and Budgie were led off to the railway police station, to the accompaniment of fulsome denunciation from the robbed citizen, the fat lady, and a character in a beret who, all shrieking at the same time, fulminated and impugned.

Word came back that Dove and Budgie had gone down for three years apiece. Hot property from the sports store was found when their homes were searched. The police pulled in the Azerbaidzhani fence while they were at it. The conventions of the criminal underworld would ensure Dove and Budgie had a hard time in the juvenile offenders' prison for having fingered him.

Skunk got through his eighth year of schooling and was duly awarded his place at the technical college. Zhenka went off to the country to stay with her grandmother. He thought he would put his lean-to to rights again and spend the summer by the river, but that was before the incident with the parka.

11

At just this moment Skunk's mother, full apparently of the joys of spring, hit the bottle with such a vengeance that she ended up in hospital. Two days after having her stomach pumped and her body injected full of drugs she was convulsed and incapable of keeping anything down. Her blotchy red hands shook helplessly, as indeed did the rest of her, and she groaned dreadfully, cursing the demon vodka and scared witless by the paramedic who had resuscitated her telling her for a fact that it was only a matter of time before she croaked. Ampoules of nikethamide, phials of valocordin, and tablets of vitamin C were piled on her bedside table, and a pungent smell of hospitals pervaded the flat. His mother got up only to stagger through to the bathroom to purge herself of her poisons. There she would crash about, gasping and wailing and, sodden and unkempt, in only her nightdress, with a quilted jacket thrown over her shoulders, shuffle back to bed, reassuring herself in a breaking, hoarse whisper, "There, there now, it's all getting better". But never before had she been this violently ill. In the past, even if she had had to hold the tumbler in a towel in order not to drop it, even if her teeth had rattled against the glass, she had had another little drink and managed, if with difficulty, to keep it down. Though her insides recoiled, this put the colour back in her cheeks, eased her breathing, picked her up and got her back to work again, out to the streets and on to another tincture and another drinking spree for as long as her money and health held out. But now she was unmistakably ill, and spent the whole of May trying to climb back out, refusing hospitalization and purging herself the traditional way, with honey which Raissa brought and leaves of mountain cranberry, until by the beginning of summer she had come back to life, relaxed a bit, and started drinking again, only beer this time, only lousy, harmless beer, just for her heart; and she seemed once again, little by little, little something by little something, to be slipping into another cycle of joyless dependence, from which the next step was begging in the gutter, a final loss of identity, and relapse into a state of blurred timelessness.

While she was ill she needed Skunk to fetch and carry, bear witness to her constant suffering, and just be a living, breathing presence by her side. He even became her Danilush-ka, her baby boy, her only little treasure. But no sooner was she on the mend than she pulled away from him again, the shutters came down, and the shrieking started all over again. Her nerves were in tatters, as neglected as the tangled hair on her head which had long forgotten what it was to be gathered up into a bun.

Vasya was washed into their home on the wave of her lousy, harmless beer. He was a digger driver thrown out by his family, who dreamed of starting a new life. When he had imbibed Vasya became mawkishly caring, bringing first cakes and chocolate, then later on champagne and brandy, and finally, hoping to curry favour with both of them at once, but more especially with Daniil who managed only a grudging "Cheers" through his teeth when they met, he brought a Japanese parka, reduced to three hundred roubles in the offices of the factory workshops. Modishly khaki, equipped with a multiplicity of pockets and a detachable fur lining, girded with corded silk and sporting a hood, with popper buttons and a zip with special fasteners which could do up or do down as its owner fancied, this was a parka to kill for. Daniil said a loud "Cheers, mate", reconciling himself to his mother's latest if not fully, then at least sufficiently for the establishing of relations. He ran out to the hallway mirror to see how it fitted. It was really cool, a designer label adorning the breast pocket and an anchor neatly embroidered in orange thread on the shoulder.

His mother had her own views on all this and came down on Vasya like a ton of bricks, calling him every name under the sun. For Chrissakes, three hundred roubles was two months' salary and this was all he could think to do with it? Three hundred roubles and who'd he blown it on? A shitty snot-nose. Three fucking hundred roubles, she shrieked, getting off on her own hysteria before finally bursting into tears of rage.

This was more than Skunk was going to take. Just as he was, resplendent in the anorak, he ran down into the street, slept the night on some old rags in his pumping station basement, and in the morning took the parka to market, where it was snapped up. The Azerbaidzhani traders peeled off four hundred roubles and the parka was gone, leaving behind only a memory, a lingering sensation of something warm and snug caressing his body, the elegant rustling in his ears of its Japanese material... but what can mere words express?

As evening fell he went back home to find his mother and Vasya sitting in the kitchen working their way through a bottle while potatoes sizzled in lard in the frying pan. Without a word he handed Vasya three hundred roubles and, still wordless, made to go to his room.

"Oh no you don't. Not so fast!" His mother was after him

in an instant, spinning him round by the shoulder and giving his face a loud, stinging slap as she did so.

"Uncle Vasya buys him an anorak and what does he do? You little shit! How dare you?" She seemed about to tear him to pieces.

Skunk wriggled free, rushed to the front door and was away down the stairs.

"Just wait till you come back, just you wait, sonny boy," his mother shrieked at his retreating form.

He spent one night and then another in his basement. He lit up the stove but did not close the little door, staring dully, fixedly into the flames. The light flickered on his flat skunk-like snout as he sat there on a block of wood, sucking his thumb, and himself looking like a tree stump or some fanciful dysfunctional root.

Within two days he had picked some more pockets, bought a coarse quilted jacket, a pair of trousers, a heavy cotton shirt, a stout pair of rubber boots, a waterproof cape, a hand-axe, a frying pan, a clasp-knife, a skein of twine, a packet of candles, a kilogram each of salt and sugar, some tea, a plastic bottle of oil, some flour, two loaves of black bread, an idiotic-looking fur hat with a leather top in case of severe frost, three pairs of woolly stockings, a scarf and a polo-necked sweater. It was all rather bulky, and his rucksack, stuffed full and bulging, bumped awkwardly between his shoulders.

Early in the morning he was already on the outskirts of town, beyond the outpost of the traffic police. He made no attempt to hitch a lift, walking along the roadside, heading steadily northwards. He knew where he was making for. His wide nostrils flared, indicative both of indomitable character and a sturdy pair of lungs, and through them he noisily breathed in the raw fragrance of the roadside vegetation.

He soon turned off the tarmac, first on to a wet country road, then along a muddy lane, before simply striking out through the forest, which was both more agreeable and less conspicuous. He didn't force the pace, free now as a bird and with all the time in the world. If he liked he could walk the grassy footpath at the edge of an emerald field of oats, or sit a while in a hollow or a windy birch grove, or bask in a suntrap in an aromatic pine plantation. He could spread his quilted jacket on the ground and lie flat on his stomach, his arms under his chin on a bed of pine needles which smelled of mint. He could pull his boots off and rest among the ants and butterflies in an unmown meadow covered with dandelions and clover, and listen to the gentle rustling of a world that was green and young. He slept without fear, in the forest or in weather-beaten sheds or old abandoned and half-dismantled peasant huts which smelled of sheepskins and damp cinders, but never sought shelter from his fellow human beings.

He was not penniless, but frugal, buying the occasional loaf of heavy home-baked bread for a few kopeks. More often he would circle human habitation like his relative the polecat, scenting his prey and then at night, soundlessly, delighting in every minute, sneak into the chicken coop, wring the necks of the skinny, moulting hens, and bound off almost doubled up into the woods and far away, his keen night vision finally coming into its own. With his mission accomplished he would briskly put a dozen miles behind him. Wet bushes lashed his body with cold, stinging dew, but he just frowned and concentrated on steadily distancing himself from the scene of the crime. There was no following him. He took care to leave no tracks, always thinking where to tread and how. He dissolved into thin air. Dogs sent after him refused to take the scent and raised their hackles and whimpered in fear, so that not infrequently his faultlessly executed depredations were taken to be the work of a long dormant house-sprite, so deftly and, to the rustic mind, unfathomably did he gain his subsistence. One time he stole a billy goat and dragged the bug-eyed old monster behind him on a rope for a full two days, beating the dumb brute on its angular rump and driving it on without respite before cutting its throat in a quiet wood beside a brook as he had seen the village men dispatch his grand-mother's animals.

He peeled the hide off unceremoniously, knowing he could not use it, and wrapped the tongueless head in it, the hooves, the long blue rope of the intestines, the frothy crimson lungs and pungent kidneys, and buried the lot under a fir tree next to an anthill. By morning a teeming path of industrious insects led to and from the burial site. He butchered the meat, put it in a well washed polythene fertilizer sack he had picked up for the purpose, and submerged it in the stream overnight. The water leached off the blood and washed away the acrid goaty smell. Come morning he salted the flesh, wrapped it in another sack, and strapped it to the top of his rucksack. That night he baked the heart and tongue in the embers of his campfire to eat on the journey, and lightly roasted the liver and ate it, still oozing blood, straight away as a treat.

Two nights later, when the liver was finished and the meat thoroughly salted, he erected a shelter of alder branches, cut the meat into thin strips and cured it, securely sealing the entrance with more branches. He gave it two more days. He had everything worked out. He had far to travel, and no intention of going hungry. His actions were carefully gauged and schooled, as if he had done all this before. In fact, how-ever, what had to be done was not all that complicated, and suggested itself partly from what he had heard in the past, and partly from what his imagination provided. The meat ended up the colour of squashed bilberries and as tough as old boots. Just the job.

He was economical with his own provisions. When travelling

through inhabited areas he preferred to get by on other people's. People had taken plenty from him, and he was just recovering what he was owed. He didn't overdo it. The little head which had been so taxed by adding and subtraction now functioned with analytical precision, and he was instinctively frugal and purposeful.

By early July he had covered a fair distance and the forest was denser, although only intermittently. Everywhere he found it chewed away by logging operations. Idiotic cuttings leading nowhere were clogged with brushwood and good building timber, with wrecked machinery and abandoned ramshackle trailers the lumberjacks had occupied, in which he was well content to spend the night. Failing that, he would snuggle down in the hollow between the roots of a fir tree, having first lined it with young branches, leaves and dry grass. He would spread his groundsheet over this bedding, pull on his quilted jacket and, if it was cold and damp, wrap himself in his blanket and fall asleep. The summer nights were light, so he slept little, just two or three hours from force of habit. He would have a bite to eat and doze some more while his footwear and clothes dried out by the fire. Then he was up again as the coolness of the hour before dawn triggered an invisible spring in his body and drove him on further north into the real wilds.

Ever more often his path was crossed by animal tracks. Sometimes the elk droppings were still steaming, and he saw the dark patches of wild boars' lairs in the peatbogs marked by piles of uprooted moss. At night he heard stirrings and gruntings nearby but heeded them little: where there were wild animals there were at least no human beings. The landscape began to change, and he often crunched through areas devastated by forest fires and subsequently colonized by lichen, white moss, and waxy cowberries. The birds of the pine forest were increasingly tame. He also came upon hunters' cabins, empty now until winter, and thus acquired a billy-can,

44

an enamel mug, and a supplement to his supply of salt. That was the best he could do: anything more useful the occupants had prudently taken home, safe from intruders like himself.

He gave any small towns and villages a wide berth, detecting their nearness from the all-pervading smell of petrol and sudden pitted tarmac roads and electricity lines cutting through the expanse of countryside. He got by on what he could plunder from the smallest villages which, for all their poverty, were replete with simple, filling food which was his for the taking. In one such he scored a major success, or rather carried through something he had planned without knowing exactly when and where he would strike lucky, although fairly sure that sooner or later he would.

Hiding in the burdocks by the village boundary he settled down to watch the comings and goings of the owners of the nearest house. They were getting ready for a journey, and were darting around the yard carrying and fetching. The mistress of the house took down the washing, big florid dresses, little florid dresses, and hurried into the house, presumably to iron them. Her daughter, a girl of about thirteen, was lending a hand. She was slender and tall and her breasts had yet to develop; her long, flaxen hair bounced up and down as she walked, and she had a serious, responsible look to her. She was nice to her mother and even to the little brother who was running round and round the yard in circles, shrieking his head off in anticipation of whatever it was they were preparing to do.

The man of the house, when he had ritually lain for a while under the car, got to his feet, wiped his oily hands on a rag, patted his daughter on the cheek, shushed at the little monster, and then stood with legs apart holding out his hands for the girl to pour water over them from a ladle. He grunted and stamped his feet and generally revelled in washing himself at great length. Skunk watched, entranced by their companionable working and playing together. Perhaps for

45

the first time in his life the envy and ill-will gnawing at him receded, and he felt a kind of euphoria as if he were one of them. The sister and her awful little brother, the mother whose strictness was so obviously put on and the very correct father who by now was wearing a stiff-looking jacket and accepting a broad (florid) tie from the hand of his daughter all together caught him up in their infectious good humour. The man was having trouble with his tie; his daughter laughingly moved in to help, and tied the knot deftly. Skunk could suddenly feel nimble young fingers on his own chest. He was overwhelmed for a moment and the colour rushed to his cheeks. He pressed himself down to the ground, to the very roots of the weeds, and savoured their fresh smell, afraid to raise his head in case he might disrupt and lose this stolen moment.

Sure enough, when he did look up again everything had dissolved, to be replaced by a quite different scene, the way the weather sometimes changes in front of your eyes. Now they were loading the car, carrying out supplies of food and bundles of belongings. Mother was installed in the front seat while the last of the luggage was brought out by the father and daughter. Even the little monster was lugging something that was obviously far too heavy for him but which he was going to carry anyway, proudly clutching it in front of him and staggering along on his wobbly little legs. The girl had mean-while put on a dress with white frills which instantly transformed her into a detestable schoolgirl, and made her look stupid and bossy and over-serious like her mother. Skunk closed his eyes tight and again saw her knotting her father's tie and felt better. His retentive memory replayed the image, and he even relived the sense of lightheartedness. Now he watched with equanimity as they got into the car, slammed the doors, and drove out of the compound. He didn't move for a long time, his instinct bidding him stay exactly where he was.

The house stood empty until evening. At night, when the dogs had fulfilled their daily quota of barking, he broke in and found just what he was looking for: a twelve bore long-barrelled shotgun exactly like the one Uncle Kolya used to have, and a pack of ammunition to go with it. Lighthearted memories were one thing, but here at last was a stroke of real luck. He gleefully pictured to himself how upset the gun's owner would be, and the efforts his family would make to console him, specially that girl in her strict dress with the frills. He suppressed his malice, sniggered, and buggered off out the window.

By now his pack was weighing a good forty-five pounds, and that was without the long, awkward shotgun. Most of the time he carried it in his arms in front of him like a pole. He had no cause to fear winter now. He welcomed the prospect of finding himself alone with the trees, the game, the air and the stars. He took in the high, star-flecked vault of heaven, the property of no man, and tucked it away, like everything else he saw fit to appropriate, in the store room of his mind. For some reason the midges and mosquitoes left him alone, whether because of some special scent he gave off or because his grandmother had hexed his blood. Whatever the reason, it was the saving of him; without which life in these boggy northern climes would have been a slow, excruciating torment.

Skunk walked on, rejoicing as he noticed signs that the climate was growing more rigorous. Now there was a smell of water in the air, of cold and mustiness and pungent bog plants. The clouds grew denser and the rain, when it caught him, fell in piercing, merciless torrents; short, furious discharges accompanied by thunder and lightning. The trees grew thinner now, less tall, and he came across many which had been uprooted by hurricanes: their shallow roots spread far out under the moss were a sure sign that the ground here did not thaw out in the short summer. There were ever more bogs and, with them, ever more duck, teal, and sandpipers; and dying lakes choked with weed. He had reached a land of brooks and burns meandering between low banks, with speckle-finned grayling on pebbly riverbeds and dragonflies hovering above streams overgrown with currant, raspberry, and bramble bushes, bordered by impenetrable dogrose thickets and blocked by fallen trees. The tussocky ground, carpeted with soft moss only where conifers grew, slowed him down: he was covering only five to ten miles a day, as he knew from counting the number of steps he took. The last signs of human habitation disappeared. For close on a week he followed animal runs, and when finally he came to a long lake with winding shores, where in prehistoric times the earth had sunk beneath the pressure of an advancing glacier, and when he beheld a pair of swans on it and the tracks of a deer on the bluish clay at the water's edge, and beyond that and a little to one side the pawprints of some cautious member of the cat family, perhaps a wolverine, he knew he had arrived, and that if this was not the place, then it was somewhere nearby, the place he had dreamed of, the place he had seen in the flickering flames of the little stove in the basement of that faraway pumping station such a very long time ago.

The lake was walled in from every direction by a dense forest of pines and firs, dark, intense, brooding, ancient, and relieved only here and there by insets of birch trees and the occasional shimmering manes of aspens. It was a real forest, untouched as yet by screeching bandsaws and stinking logging tractors, and if a helicopter clattered overhead, at least it was headed even further north, towards the tundra and the Arctic Ocean. Man was everywhere, but here, hidden away hundreds of miles from anywhere, was a land he had seen in a vision, cut off, endowed with berries and red-capped mushrooms and wild animals, and with a singular, ringing silence that made his spine tingle.

13

He sank down on the sturdy trunk of a fallen fir tree, resting his back on its thick branches, and dug his feet into the rustling moss. He suddenly felt how tired he was. The sheer repetitive slog of his trek, all part of a single forward urge, had attuned him to pounding mechanically onwards; but now that it was over, his legs reacted, his strained eyes stung; his stamina, in whichever recess of the brain it was stored, ran out. His abdominals ached, his stomach sank, his aching, creaking joints could barely bend, his windblown, chilled, kippered, long unwashed body tingled and itched, a structure of lean muscle pricked by shooting pains, exhausted now by new, sweet, agonizing freedom. He slept.

Just as he was, sitting upright, he slept insensate through two nights and days, warm in his quilted jacket, wrapped in his blanket, sheltered from the dew by his groundsheet, unmoving and unaffected even by the basic calls of nature. A brood of hazel grouse grew accustomed to him and fearlessly pecked the mountain cranberries right beside his boots; an inquisitive squirrel, the forest rat that does its scurrying up in the trees, perched brazenly on his head, and squeaked and scampered up the nearest tree to hide in its crown only when a pair of the ubiquitous ravens swooped in and landed on nearby tree stumps. The black necrophages goggled searchingly and at length at the body in the blanket, readying themselves, blinking, a bluish membrane sliding over their eyes, but before they could make up their minds to take a peck he grunted loudly in his sleep and sent the startled snoopers about their business.

At last, as the second day was drawing to its close, he came to, straightened and stretched his heavy limbs and, long and leisurely, cracked every sinew, spreading wakefulness to every part and banishing all trace of lethargy. Then he went down to the lake to wash his face, rinse out his mouth, and drink his fill. He gathered firewood, lit a fire, and right there by the fallen tree trunk made up his bed as usual, boiled up some millet in the billy-can and ate the porridge with a chunk of hard bread, alternating this with a bite of salted goat meat. He drank a mug of sweet tea, not stinting on the sugar in honour of the occasion. He blew on the steaming tea, warmed his hands on the mug, and drank and drank and drank. Then he settled himself comfortably by the warm fire and looked out into the night, down to the quicksilver surface of the lake spread at his feet, up to the Creator's dome far overhead, across to the black stockade of trees on the meandering shoreline, and back to his crimson fire and its crumbling, hissing wood ash. And so he met his first dawn on the lake.

Before daybreak the ducks had flown in in search of new feeding grounds, followed by the seagulls, this season's large grey youngsters and mature white veterans, the seabirds again confirming that he had come far north, almost to the ocean. On the far side of the lake he spied wood grouse on a sand spit gobbling grit; then, quite near, he heard something larger than a squirrel, a pine marten perhaps, scraping its claws on bark as it passed above him. Uncle Kolya knew and loved the northern forests, and surely it must be from him that he had his love of this place and his ready knowledge of its lore.

A south-easter blew up, rippling the lake and making it impossible to see how the pike and perch were biting, but even so he could tell that their lashing tails had the whole surface simmering. From every side came the scream of break-fasting seagulls. Somewhere to the right, perhaps in an unseen inlet, a grebe hiccupped startlingly, and drew an immediate response from the swans. These imperiously brooked no intruders and gave voice to their displeasure on the least pretext or indeed none at all, proclaiming their presence and querulously trumpeting their rights of sovereignty.

He threw more wood on the fire, brewed up, and break-fasted on dried bread and more goat meat, but hurriedly now, with none of the leisurely gourmandizing of the night before. He scoured the remains of the porridge from the pan and doused the embers of the fire. It was time to find somewhere to stay.

14

For a couple of hours he followed an animal run which wound through the lakeside trees. These were shrewd animals which knew how to make themselves invisible from the lake behind the tree trunks while still enjoying a perfect view of the lake and shore opposite. Twice his eye fell on fishermen's canes which had supported nets, and he came upon the site of a campfire. The lake was inhabited by man, which did not suit him at all; but as this was his only way north he moved on guardedly, ready to dart into the thickets at any moment.

The track led him to a bog studded with high yellow tussocks. He had no option but to go down into the water and wade his way across the swampy clay bottom. At the far side a rivulet flowed into the bog from a small round lake, and beyond the stream on a high, bare mound were some buildings: a long low hut with a tarred roof, a shed, and what appeared to be a bathhouse. Steps led down to a wooden platform at the water's edge and beside them leaned a structure with poles for drying fishing nets. It stood to reason: a lake as large and productive as this one was bound also to have a permanent fishing brigade working it. Next Skunk saw the helicopter pad marked out by four barrels, and an aerial wire threading its way from the house to the top of a pole from which a faded Soviet flag flapped dispiritedly.

He sat down gingerly on a tussock, puzzled by the complete absence of any smell of occupancy. No smoke came from the chimney, and there was no boat at the moorings, although a dinghy and a skiff lay keel uppermost on the bank. He waited until dusk and, when nobody showed up, waded across the river and crept cautiously up to the house.

The boats were lying near an open dug-out for gutting fish. It was full of barrels, all empty except for one which was full of caked grey salt crystals. There were no fresh fish scales and no glistening tracks on the wet path up to the house. There had been nobody here for several months; the yard in front of the hut was strewn with duck feathers.

Inside the house reeked of paraffin soot and the dust of neglect. Skunk lit a candle. They had left a lot of stuff behind: more, indeed, than he could possibly have hoped for. In a long scullery were an iron cooking stove, cupboards which were far from bare, containing tins of cereal, a bottle of cooking oil, a whole sack of sugar, packets of tea, matches, and candles, all nibbled by the mice, two paraffin lamps with a box of spare glass panels to go with them, buckets, saucepans and frying pans, bowls and mugs, glasses, two axes and a hatchet, a two-handed and a single-handed saw, and a can of paraffin. In the living section were a brick stove, four broad sleeping benches along the walls, a table in the middle, and a tiny window. Under the table he found a pair of entirely serviceable felt boots and some worn-out shoes, evidently used as house slippers; the benches even came complete with matresses, blankets and pillows.

Skunk got the stove going. His provident fishermen had chopped a wide stack of firewood and left a great pile of logs, cut with a mechanical saw, for idle hands with a hatchet. He reckoned there was wood enough for a year or more. To one side was a leaning bathhouse in the entrance to which he found some clean empty whitewood barrels they had used for keeping bread. He mentally allocated them for storing berries.

In the morning he found any number of new wonders. The boats were wholly seaworthy, and in the dug-out he found tar, green paint and a can of drying oil to stop leaks. In the attic there were two spades, a pickaxe and, best of all, some perfectly usable fishing nets.

For the first week he toiled like a man possessed, cleaning the house of mouse droppings, sorting the cereals, the salt and paraffin, arranging everything to his liking on the shelves, and washing the crockery. He launched the skiff and set up the fishing nets at the nearest buoys. The fishermen had removed only their radio equipment, the petrol saw, the outboard motors, and a motorbike, signs of which he found in the empty shed. It was clear enough that they had left their gear because they intended coming back, but that was now hardly likely to be this year. In a month or two the lake would freeze over and if there was fishing to be done it was now or never. Evidently something urgent had led to their abandoning the autumn fishing season.

Having put his house in order, he stoked up the stove in the bathhouse, even finding two bars of brown household soap and two partly used cakes of toilet soap. He gave himself a good steaming and scraped away the grime; then he gave his sweat impregnated, smoky clothes a thorough laundering. And then he went to bed and slept until he could sleep no more, and became aware for the first time in many weeks that he had hair, and skin which smelled agreeably, and which was soft and pleasant to touch.

His new life gave him all the space in the world, but not enough time, all of which went on preparing for winter. First thing in the morning Skunk was out in the skiff checking his nets and harvesting the fish: pike, perch, burbot, roach, the silvery houting, and any grayling that had strayed out from their streams; he gutted and salted them in the trough. Then he would brew up some tea, drink the soup he had made the night before, and be off to the forest in search of berries. Cranberries went straight into their barrel; bilberries he rolled in a blanket to separate out the leaves, moss, and other forest detritus, before covering them with water and leaving them to steep. He dredged brambles and currants in sugar and stored them in jars, of which he had found a great quantity in the store room. He dried rose hips and mushrooms over the cooker, alternating the amber coloured strings with what looked like strings of jet black rosary beads for effect. When he was out in the woods he would shoot any wood grouse or black-cock foolish enough to offer themselves up. There was an abundance of these, so he did not waste shot on the diminutive hazel grouse.

Each evening he would sort the fish, each variety going into its own barrel ready for the winter. His net was catching well enough, but he set another two nearby, one barring the mouth of the stream, and the other suspended between stakes he found already in place beside a reed-covered sandbank. These were very productive, as the fishing collective had evidently discovered.

Before turning in for the night he did the rounds of his domain, inspecting his accumulating supplies. If the rightful owners were to return unexpectedly he would be able to face them unashamed, with a full larder. He hoped, however, that they would not return, and with every passing day became increasingly confident that the hope was justified. He was the undisputed master of the lake, he and the pair of swans which met his skiff with furious hissing and did not allow it within range for a shot. Along the shores wandered deer and elk, and he saw the droppings of a bear and happened more than once on its great heavy pawprints; but bears keep out of sight, and Skunk was in no hurry to seek it out, or any of the other larger animals for that matter. There was game in plenty to keep him fully occupied.

In the evenings, before the sun set, he would go out to a high mound by the lakeside to sit on a bench he had put there specially. At such moments the world around and he seemed a single entity. What was inside him and what extended there outside him seemed to fuse without resistance into a harmonious space full of a pulsing, sacramental stillness, and the dizzying contemplation of it filled his body with a joyful lightness. His

54

God-given sense of direction meant that he always knew which way was north, which south, where the sun would rise and where it would hide itself; but strangely, now that he was here and found himself somehow at the centre of all his land, because his realm had previously extended no further than his last few footsteps, he had become aware of a different, reverse link. There ran out from his bench on the mound threads which were at first invisible but later, with the passing of time, became ever more tangible; lines which had a specific scent and colour, broken and bending, straight and curving, and which snaked round to places beyond the probing of the eye, undulating and consolidating into a single great, dome, like a gigantic water melon which enveloped the earth and, entranced, he raised a finger and traced the angular line of the tops of the fir trees, the billowing, changeful clouds, the foot of the forest, and rocks far and near, as if, but no, he actually was outlining them, sketching them; and it seemed as though in a moment, when he had done enough, he would roll up the finished sketch, tuck it into his shirt front, take it home with him to the hut and keep it all to himself. But that was not it. He knew that with his tracing he was not seeking possession, but only to mark, as a beast does, his territory, to stake it out and establish himself there for real, and sometimes, in a great, crazy access of joy, he would suddenly break out in a yell, "Aaaaah!", and the echo would multiply his shout and return it. The swans on the water would look about them startled, beat their wings on the taut surface of the lake, and take themselves off to a remote part; there they would seek temporary refuge behind a promontory, only to sail back later with the wind behind them, to eye with sanctimonious resentment the eccentric intruder in their world whose insolence appeared to know no bounds.

Everything in his environment became part of him: the life immediately to hand, the sedge, rushes, the perch leaping in the lake, the tiddlers darting over the stones, the osiers in the bog, the mighty fir trees on the shores, all of it primal and fragrant; the breeze, the rain, the mushrooms sprouting, the great red-caps sometimes the size of a pudding basin, solid and cold but themselves a wholly insignificant part of an underground mycelium which extended for half a mile, its rooftop sentries dispatched to the surface to scatter spores and continue the species; and somewhere a bear, unseen but quite certainly keeping an eye on him from some vantage point, and the hypersensitive deer with their foolish eyes. This all-engulfing feeling called not for explanation but for a living into the stillness ringing somewhere behind the ear, for a dissolving of all in each and of each in all, for self-forgetful thanksgiving: it was the total self-sufficiency of living beings, with no domination, no needless prettifying, where everything was made more beautiful by everything else, everything was dominant and everything was subordinate, where everything cooperated in symbiosis, instinctively, in accordance with a simple and unchallengeable order.

In a moment of fevered, half-delirious insight he felt rather than thought that in taking up his part in this he was finally acquitted of plundering, acquitted because of his complicity, his sharing in creating and breathing that stillness for which, perhaps, the subterranean ramifications of a mycelium or a little bush of black baneberry were of greater import than his figure sitting hunched on its bench.

Having sat in this state until the night was inky black or until he was driven away by a chill wind, he would go off to bed, bolting the door, putting more wood in the stove, putting out the lamp. His dreams were a continuation of the forest, the lake, the boggy landscape, and differed little from what he saw during the working day. But one time the forgotten past became entangled.

That day he had really exhausted himself hauling a gigantic sixty-five pound pike out of the nets. He had first to beat its head with the axe butt for ages and then, attaching it by the eye sockets, to unmesh it from the net and drag it on board. He got completely covered in fish slime, and after that had to fillet the brute, and salt it piece by piece, almost filling a whole barrel.

It was this pike that re-appeared in his dream, talking like the golden fish in Pushkin's fairy tale. He had paddled out deep into the lake to wash when up swam the pike, looked out of the water at him, spoke, and invited him to tea. Without a moment's hesitation he set off after it, knee-deep, waist-deep, up to his chin. The water did not feel cold or even wet his clothing. He climbed on to the pike's back the way in the village he used to sit on the back of a piglet, and the fish swam down with him to the depths of the lake where it lived in a kind of homely underwater den. It was warm and dry there. The pike poured from a copper kettle an infusion which looked like tea made from seaweed and river plants. It was an improbable violet colour. He gazed raptly into the cup as if it were a mirror, and in it saw Zhenka and his mother in a bathhouse, naked and splashing about in a green swimming pool. Then his mother got out on to the side and while Zhenka was ecstatically kicking out with her arms and legs like a frog, she poured something into the water from a tub. It must have been a potion of some kind, because Zhenka instantly turned into a hideous monster. From her sides and abdomen grew three dogs' heads, stinking, howling, and vomiting out a poisonous venom. His mother gave a shriek of horror and disappeared. Zhenka, however, moved to the shallow end, raised her arms and, swaying her hips as if dancing, started to rock the dogs to calm them down. They quietened gradually, but now they were no longer dogs. She was ensnared by three bodies which had grown together with hers: Moose, Budgie and Dove. They started nipping and biting her, but Zhenka seemed remote from it all, evidently feeling no pain. The three of them seemed to be doing their best to topple her. Each of the legless monsters was reaching out to touch her breasts, pushing aside the lascivious hands of its rivals. Now they were all shrieking frenziedly, "Me, me! She's mine, mine". But then from the side of the swimming pool he, Skunk, swam up with a trailing crown of green seaweed on his head. They stared at him and were struck dumb.

"She is mine," he said, flashed his eyes menacingly, and waded over to Zhenka. The gang vanished by magic in an instant. Zhenka threw up her arms as if she too was being carried away, and the tableau disappeared.

He was back in the pike's lair and his hostess, old and kind, in some way now reminded him of his grandmother. The pike insistently urged him to take a sip of the tea.

He had a vague foreknowledge that the infusion would taste good, as children can have, not rationally but from something deep and strange, and took a gulp. The liquid had no taste, but his body was suffused with serenity. He turned into a fish god, complete with scales and webbed hands and feet. The pike crowned him with a fine fur hat with floppy ear flaps. Time ceased to exist. He achieved a state of bliss.

He woke up amazed. The dream had both frightened and relaxed him, recalling the past but also reconciling him with the present. Meditatively sucking his thumb, he went out for a pee and suddenly realized that his jet was leaving its mark on white snow. Snowflakes were falling soundlessly from the sky. With no hint of wind, winter was closing in.

15

The snow did not lie: it was washed away by cold, lashing rain. Then more snow fell and the rain again washed it away. Winter was taking the earth with guerilla tactics. The swans joined the flocks of birds calling in the sky and were the last to fly off, after the seagulls and the ducks, after all the lake's lesser breeds had left frantically beating the air with their wings. The lake iced over thinly, and in the cove the ice could even take the weight of a man, but each time a strong north wind came along to break it up. Towards evening the ice would begin to crack and snap, and break up into long sections. The air creeping under it first made it bulge and then rushed out to the surface with wild, almost animal howling. During the night the north wind would fragment the floes into tiny pieces, and piles of sharp, glinting shards would be washed up on the shore. During the day the foul west wind blew, bringing warm fronts and piling up thunderclouds as far as the eye could see. Really bad weather set in. The wind and rain drove the game of the pinewoods away from the beaches to seek shelter beneath the branches in the thick of the forest. His catches of fish were poor, the bilberry bushes almost bare, the hazel grouse did not whistle in the mornings waiting for fair weather. The rowans shook their locks above the water like red grapeshot.

The rains brought boredom and depression in their wake. He moved about unwillingly, lethargically, took down two of the nets, leaving only the first, most productive one. He chopped all the logs and made a new woodpile, set traps for hazel grouse on the shores, remembering lessons learned from Uncle Kolya. It was very easy: you erected a low barrier of twigs on the sandy beaches and left only a few little gates, also low, and just wide enough for an inquisitive hen to stick her head through. Above the gate you placed a birch bough wound with nylon thread, and dangled a noose from it. Your wood grouse marched on to the beach in search of grit, noticed the strange obstacle and, without pausing for thought, pattered straight over to the gap and shoved its neck in the noose. Occasionally the bird might manage to drag the pole off into the forest, but more often it sat their dejected and alone on the windy beach, peering in dislike and fear at Skunk as he approached.

The traps needed to be checked every day. Take your eye off the ball and you would find only down and feathers: the pine martens did their best to get there first. Sometimes the ravens would descend on a strangled wood grouse, and he would arrive to find them in mid-feast and would then have to spend a lot of time, cursing all their tribe, painstakingly sweeping away the traces, and gathering up every scrap of the down and feathers scattered far and wide over the beach before burying it all out of sight and levelling the sand off to a virginally pure state once more.

The approach of winter turned the squirrels' fur snowy white, and stripped the birch trees of their golden leaves. The forest turned into a black strip with occasional blotches of scarlet where the aspen trees were still resisting, and saffron yellow patches where bogs smelling of sodden, rotting hay still had the low-growing osiers fighting back and holding on to their slender leaves. For all that, winter was closing in day by day. The snow finally settled, and it was comical to see at one of the now rare sunny noontides a many-legged karamor stumbling about on it, and the beige moths with their enormous eyes which had mistaken the season, and woken suddenly to dance out what remained of their day in the bright harsh rays. He had to cosset his feet in an extra layer of wrappings, for which he ripped up an old blanket. But the snow also made tracking easier. The hares were driven out of the depths of the forest, and Skunk set snares on their runs too.

He made a cold store in the shed and kept the plucked wood grouse and skinned hares in there. Having nothing better to do, Skunk hit on the idea of making himself a crude winter coat by facing his thoroughly draughty quilted jacket with their fur. In the long evenings he sat in the fumes of the paraffin lamp, fleshing his skins, stretching them on boards, and hanging them up by the ceiling to dry. Finally he took down the last net, cutting it out of the ice, dragged the skiff up on to the bank and even erected a covering over it. Such minor chores of this kind helped to fill his time, but the clouds obscuring the sun and the early darkness made him feel very low.

Towards the end of October the weather settled at last. The wood grouse colonized the pine woods by the lake, drawn to it like moths to a flame to forage in the shallow snow for bilberries, and would beat a noisy retreat through a gap in the trees at his approach. A drunkard husband seeking forgiveness at the weekend by carpet beating in the yard could not have made more noise than one of the cocks taking flight. Invulnerable at the top of the fir tree, silhouetted against a light sky, pop-eyed and ponderous, the bird would crane an infinitely long neck and eye the unbidden guest. Hunting the birds became an obsessional battle of wits to determine who had the better hearing and quicker reactions. After many failed attempts Skunk learned how to get within range, but shot only when he was sure of a kill, often returning home with an empty rucksack.

The lake finally froze up, which shortened his journey to the opposite shore dramatically. He put on a pair of skis, essential to survival here, and started exploring further afield.

Even so, in the evenings his throat would smart and his neck came out in gooseflesh, as if he were sitting in a draught. Taciturn since childhood, he now suddenly felt burdened by the isolation and, against all precedent, started talking to himself. The town, his mother, even Zhenka whom he had cast out of his heart could not be kept from welling up in memory like ghosts from a forgotten movie; they would glimmer insubstantially above a track, or be imagined in the profile of a growth on a birch tree; and in the howling of the wind he heard faraway voices.

It was not that he was gripped by fear; indeed he was unacquainted with that emotion. But it became clear that a hermit's life had its drawbacks. He became more and more self-absorbed. For example, he could obsessively sniff the wrinkles on his horn-like thumb at inordinate length; scrutinize the hairs on his hand minutely, pluck at the mop of hair on his head with an idiot, otherworldly look on his face; or rub the dead skin on his foot methodically, roughly, in time to the faint singing of the stove...

One bright, frosty morning he set off early on his skis, gliding down the mound on to the ice and pushing on far to the north, across bogs and a long swamp, over an unfamiliar river and into the beginnings of the tundra. In its all-enveloping silence he shot two white ptarmigans, and on the way back home a hen wood grouse. With a full, heavy rucksack, tired and hungry, he was climbing his mound when two huskies leaped out at him. There was someone, perhaps more than one person, in his house. He could see a heat haze shimmering above the chimney. A pair of heavy hunters' skis, crusted with ice, had been wearily stuck in the woodpile.

The obvious thing to do was go in, but his visitor beat him to it, kicking the door open, while himself standing over slightly to one side in the shadows. The paraffin lamp on the shelf breathed in the cold air, sweated and flared. By its flickering light he made out a lilac silhouette. The gun in its hands, with its threaded rifle barrel and parallel shotgun, identified a professional hunter. Steam billowed out of the house, and there was a welcoming smell of overheated fat and sweet paraffin vapour. Skunk looked more closely, and their eyes met.

16

The man was not tall, but sturdily built, his barrel chest too tight a fit for his much mended sweater. His hair was close cropped and greying, he had a small beard the size of a toy spade for the beach, a snub nose, and bushy black eyebrows from beneath which his eyes peered searchingly.

"Your dad bringing up the rear, sonny?"

"I don't have a dad, or anyone else. I'm on my own."

The man let him in, and lit up a cigarette.

"On your own, eh? Better tell me all about it, then."

62

Skunk briefly outlined how he came to be there, improving the story a bit and making himself out to be an orphan. But he did mention Stargorod.

"All the way from Stargorod, on foot?" the man repeated his words slowly, as if weighing up the information. "I noticed someone had been in, and the brigade are at Lake Ivelsky now. They were sent there back in May. How long were you planning to stay?"

"I don't know. Whatever."

"By the by, I'm Vitaly. I hunt for the State Procurement Department. Sit down, have something to eat. After that we can think how we're going to live together."

"Fine. There's plenty of food. Enough to live on," Skunk said, testing his rights to carry on living in the hut.

"That's not a problem. I have a place at Lake Gluboky, twelve miles south of here. I stay over here with the fishermen one day in every three or four. I have a triangular route of traps. I head over here one day, stay the night; next day I go over to Lake Kalitnyansky, there's a winter cabin there too; and one day I get to spend at home. Just keep going round in a circle. You snaring hares?"

"For a coat. I want to face my jacket."

"Quite the furrier. How do you tan them?"

Skunk had no answer to that. He had supposed that when you had dried the skins they were ready to use. Vitaly merely chuckled. He went out, rummaged around in the loft, and came back with two bottles of vinegar essence.

"This is what you use for tanning. What you've got there is raw skins. Go get us some water, Robinson Crusoe."

While Skunk was going down to get water from his hole in the ice, Vitaly straightened the skins out, sprinkled them generously with salt, and instructed Skunk to rub it well in on the flesh side. Then he laid them in rows in the trough, weighted them down with bricks, and submerged them in a weak solution of the vinegar.

"That's more like it. They can steep in there for a while."

After that they had a brew up. Vitaly had a big quart mug of his own and took his time, sipping the tea slowly, occasionally poking a wet finger in the sugar and licking it to sweeten the tea.

"You're not afraid of the forest, then?" He was still sizing Skunk up.

"It doesn't bother me. I'm just a bit bored being on my own. Otherwise I'm okay."

"Bored? You won't be bored in the forest. There's work to be done. Are you man for it, or are you here as a tourist?"

"I'll do it!" Skunk nodded enthusiastically. The isolation really had been getting to him.

"Off to bed then now. We'll talk all about it in the morning." Vitaly put the lamp out and was soon snoring.

Skunk, completely shattered after his day in the forest, seemed only to have been waiting to get into his warm bed, but now tossed restlessly for a long time, sucking his thumb and staring at the ceiling, trying to get his head round what had happened. He was being taken on as an apprentice, and the calm confidence of the man who was now asleep made him calm and confident too, except that he could not sleep.

In the morning Vitaly inspected his hunting equipment and appeared to find it satisfactory.

Each of the dogs received a salted fish, which they gulped down whole. Then the two men put on their skis, and Skunk also strapped on a harness for pulling the sledge, which carried a canvas bag laden with traps, wire and wire cutters. They went off to set their traps.

And so the round began, every day a hard slog which would have been totally monotonous but for the forest. From one hut to the next on a great triangular route, the forest was invariably virgin and every time quite new, full of surprises, animals, sounds.

At first the hunter gave curt explanations, showing him what was what; but Skunk was a natural and they did not talk

64

when they were on the move in the forest. They skied in silence, in silence they approached a bird the dogs were barking over and killed it for bait; in silence they retrieved a marten from a trap, regarding one skin a day as major success; they took squirrels too. When they did talk was before turning in. Vitaly would settle himself on the sleeping bench, light up a cigarette, sip his mug of tea, and tell his stories. And Skunk would listen, in no hurry to open up about his own life. Vitaly got the message and did not pry. It all worked out. They lived without upset.

17

The idyll lasted just a month or six weeks. While they were getting the measure of each other, getting used to each other's ways, everything went passably enough. The work did not get on top of him, and fetching an extra pail of water, heating up or cooking a meal was no big deal for Skunk. He hauled logs, chopped firewood, cooked meals, and waded up to his waist in snow after the game they caught. Vitaly the Hunter confined his attention to skins. He sorted them, fleshed them, dried them, counted them, and worked out how much he was going to get for them. Skunk soon gathered that Vitaly had no plans to share the proceeds. There was nothing so surprising about that: a hunter's livelihood depends on how he does in the winter. Skunk was being accommodated in Vitaly's winter quarters, had his food provided, cooked his pancakes at the the hunter's expense, ate his bacon, and munched his dried bread. In the forest that was worth a great deal. But he was also slaving his guts out with never a word of encouragement in return. Vitaly thought he should only have to explain things once, and if Skunk got the least thing wrong, he would explode, beside himself with rage. He would swear under his breath for ages afterwards, muttering as they continued on their way: "I suppose it's too much to expect the little hoodlum to tie a knot right. He's only good for tying shoe laces."

Often in the evenings Skunk would go off on his own and, grinding his teeth, set about knotting the wet, icy ends of a rope. He even dreamed of it at night. He would wake up in a cold sweat and, still drugged with sleep, rolling his eyes, start working out whether you make the loop to the right, push the end under, over the top and pull or, no... and he would fall back on the mattress and switch off.

He did get the hang of the knots, but received never a "well done" or a "thank you" for his pains. Vitaly himself had been through a hard school, and the yelling and nit-picking and endless crude swearing were a legacy of his own past superiors and tyrannical little bosses who had long since shot his nerves to pieces. He had a wife and two children living in a village somewhere up near Arkhangelsk, although where exactly Skunk did not bother to remember. Vitaly saw them only intermittently. In the summer he made a living by fishing and berry picking, and he sat out the winters in the forest. He wanted to get away from the world and, just as he berated but put up with the huskies he had working for him, so he got to treating Skunk, perhaps even marginally better.

In short, they both kept themselves to themselves and the antagonism which had developed was only beginning to undermine relations. Vitaly showed him how to sew the fur to his jacket, but left Skunk to prick his fingers with the big, crooked needle and just laughed up his sleeve. He laughed at him the first day and a second, but finally took pity and made him a tin thimble. It seemed like an act of charity, but why had he taken so long to do it? Skunk didn't forget that. He didn't forget anything.

Skunk liked to sit in the evenings looking out of the little window into the dark. Vitaly couldn't stand idle hands, and went out of his way to find him something, anything to do. One time when the ice glazed forest was dancing outside the window, he told Skunk to bring in more firewood.

"Sod off. I've just got warm," Skunk retorted.

66

"Who are you telling to sod off? Do you expect me to do it?" Vitaly roared, turning red as a beetroot. He dragged Skunk off his bunk, overturning a table in the process, and gave him a slap to his head which sent him flying over to the door.

"No answering back in the fleet, right? You'll behave the way my father taught me to behave. Out!"

Skunk did not move.

"Get up when I say so!"

"You are not my father," Skunk said, finally getting to his feet. He went over to the door and took his fur covered jacket off the hook. He put it on, collected his mug and his gun, fastened on his ammunition belt, and slipped into the straps of his rucksack. Vitaly watched in silence.

"Thank you for your hospitality, your bread and salt. You are not my father. Okay?" Skunk repeated.

"Have you taken leave of your senses? Where the hell do you think you're going at this time of night. Cool it!" The hunter decided to sue for peace, but Skunk went outside. Vitaly ran out after him with his gun.

"I bear you no grudge, but I've had enough of slogging my guts out for you. I'll live as I did before. If you want to visit, feel free."

"You're crazy. Hold it right there! I won't allow you to go into the forest at night!"

"There's a moon," Skunk said, jabbing a finger heavenwards. "Shoot if you want to." He headed off towards the forest.

"You goat! You stupid, motherless goat! You aren't at summer camp now, you know, sonny boy!" Vitaly raged back at the hut, trying to fight off the overexcited dogs which had just come bounding up at the wrong moment. The dogs whined.

"Come back, we'll kill an elk. We'll kill an e-elk."

The echo bandied his cry to and fro. Skunk sped back to his hut along the familiar, compacted ski track. The anger in his heart fell away instantly: he was intoxicated by the freedom. The fluttering snow was as sweet as ice cream on his lips. Four hours later he was leaning against his doorpost gasping for breath, drops of sweat chilling his forehead. The wind was cold on his cheeks; the moon and stars gave off a wild perfume. If he could, he would have howled in ecstasy!

18

Vitaly arrived towards evening the following day. He was completely covered in snow, overexcited, and making too much noise.

"Evening, Crusoe!" he shouted as if nothing had happened.

Skunk's walk-out had forced a change of attitude.

"Here, get to work on this," he said, throwing a large wood grouse on the table. "There aren't so many birds about now, are there, and the blizzards will be starting soon. Then what are you going to do?"

"Survive."

"You'll survive! Sure you'll survive. If need be you can get by on nothing but fish, but it won't be much fun with no meat, eh? Or are you going to be a hermit?"

He rattled on, hanging his wet clothes up around the stove to dry. There was a new tone in his voice, overly cheery, ingratiating. Vitaly wanted a truce.

"And something else, young whippersnapper: an elk has come over from the Koloch marshes. What say we track him down together?"

Skunk concentrated on his ladling, as if he was pouring pewter into some extremely intricate mould.

"Suit yourself, I'll get by on my own. It won't be the first time, but what an elk! It took even my breath away today, standing there like an elephant; seventeen or twenty branches on its antlers. It's not an elk, it's a bulldozer!"

Skunk silently sipped the scalding, turbid grouse broth.

Vitaly had told him before about Koloch, a region of impassable marshes which surrounded islands of forest with worn away barren clearings where ancient, craggy rocks thrust up out of the moss. It was no place for human beings. Even in the frozen depths of winter you could fall into a bubbling hole where no ice had formed. After a geologists' four-wheel drive was sucked down a few winters ago the place had come to be regarded as totally unsafe and accursed. The geologists had been looking for, and had seemingly found, uranium. His head full of newspaper horror stories, Vitaly would always conclude, "What's the point of prospecting there? Any man who went to Koloch without a leaden bollock-shield would never get it up again." He did, however, concede the place some unusual features. According to hunters' tales, the animals grew to incredible size in Koloch (obviously mutants!), and all in all, it was a daunting but tempting region. What professional hunter doesn't dream of undisturbed forests where the animals are still tame? Vitaly talked about Koloch as if it were the land of his dreams, but always made it clear that the magical place only appealed to his imagination.

"Some helicopter pilots saw smoke coming from a geologists' cabin this year. Someone living there, do you reckon?"

"How should I know?"

"Or maybe it's somebody overwintering there, or some mermaids maybe? Bet you wouldn't say no to a mermaid right now, or aren't you up to it? Cat got your tongue? A mermaid is best when you've had well over the limit. You can't have her, because there's nowhere down there to have but if you look at the little sweetie you'll swoon like a six-year-old girl looking at a dandelion, right?"

He rattled on in the same vein all evening.

That night a snowstorm set in which did not let him get away for two days. They fired up the bathhouse and steamed themselves, sprawling on the benches. Vitaly carried on spinning his yarns. He couldn't get the elk out of his mind.

"You need to go at him from two sides at once and drive him straight towards your hut..."

Skunk knew what he was on about. You pursue a wounded beast through deep, powdery snow. A wily hunter worked the route out in advance and finished the luckless animal off as near home as possible. A kind of primitive home delivery service. It would clearly be handy for Vitaly to have a hunting partner covering him, but it was also as clear as day that if Skunk joined him in this pursuit he would be back to doing Vitaly's chores, and he was having none of that.

When the snowstorm calmed down, Vitaly prepared to leave.

"Well, then. Are you coming?" He was confident he had talked Skunk round.

"Take it how you like, Vitaly. I'm not coming."

"Well now, you really are stubborn. No harm in that. I'm pretty pig-headed myself, brother. So be it. I'll be back with elk meat. You wait and see." He flashed a smile at him. "It's up to you. Take your time. Think things through. Keep smiling." Vitaly waved to him with his gun. "I'll be back two days from now."

Should he have gone with him? Vitaly had mellowed, and seemed to have a new respect for Skunk's obstinacy. No, he was doing the right thing. It would be a mistake to give in straight away. Skunk had a point to make.

But Vitaly did not show up two days later as he had promised. Indeed, early in the morning of the third day one of the huskies turned up: on its own, without its mate, and without its master. It was whimpering and fawning on Skunk, trying to get him to follow it into the forest. He got ready in haste, put on his skis, and the dog immediately rushed on ahead, clearly knowing just where it wanted to lead him. They slid down the mound and carried on three hundred yards or so through the reeds at the edge of the lake. Suddenly the dog's hackles rose and it rushed into the forest barking wildly. Skunk pulled his head down into his jacket and slowed abruptly. He heard the sound of wheezy breathing, as if someone were trying to fan the fire in a samovar with an old boot.

Beside a large juniper bush on the edge of the forest stood a gigantic elk. Its magnificent antlers were bowed almost to the ground. The beast laboriously raised its massive head, rolling back its deeply sunken, bloodshot eyes in search of the troublesome dog.

Hobbling along, its chest falling on to its forelegs and dragging one of its rear legs, the elk turned sharply to one side, presenting itself side on to Skunk. Its flanks collapsed inwards as it breathed, and pink foam bubbled on its fleshy, grey lips.

It was half dead. So this was what the dog had been leading him towards. Skunk soundlessly broke his shotgun, slipped in a bullet cartridge, and held a second in his twisted mouth. He aimed for just below the ear: a mere thirty paces separated them, but still the elk had not noticed him, snorting in agitation as it watched its tormentor frenziedly leaping about between the fir trees. He fired and hastily reloaded, but that was enough. The elk crashed down on top of the splintering juniper bush.

The husky rushed forward, growling, baring its fangs, its hackles concertinaed, but not daring to attack. It rushed around in circles, raising clouds of powdery snow. Skunk administered the coup de grâce, knowing it was already all over. The beast's ears hung listless; its great head twitched; and a dark stream of blood flowed from its brow over its eye socket.

He waited some time before approaching the warm steaming carcass. He understood now why the elk had failed to notice him. Its swollen rear leg was crusted with congealed blood where it had been shredded by shot. The elk associated danger with the barking dog, since it had been present when it was first stricken by the treacherous shot, a cartridge of which had also gone into its belly. The gigantic bull had come to the lake to die. Skunk had merely hastened the end.

Vitaly had missed his big chance and Skunk had taken it. And what a trophy this was. You could never have hauled something this size any distance. Skunk took out his knife, but the dog would give him no peace. It kept running off towards the forest, barking, coming back, running off again. He cut out the elk's tongue and wrapped it in a cloth, but the barking from the forest did not die down. He cast a glance at the snow-covered fir trees and decided to go to meet Vitaly. His head was pounding with unexpected delight.

It hadn't snowed the night before. Skunk retraced the deep, blood flecked tracks of the wounded beast. The elk had forced itself on without rest, sinking at times up to its belly in the snow, punishingly. Slightly to one side were the dark, comma-shaped pawprints of the husky. Had the clever dog been guiding him home, or had the elk taken this route itself?

By a hunter's lake, in a large swamp, Skunk read what had happened. The dogs had chased the elk out into the snow, towards Vitaly. He had loosed off with shot, beginning the pursuit. It had not lasted long, because the elk, floundering in the fresh snow and ploughing a deep furrow with its belly, had suddenly jumped up on to Vitaly's mound, sensing firm ground beneath its feet.

An area of about a hundred yards square, so completely churned up by hooves that not a single scrap of white remained, was drenched in blood and strewn with shreds of jacket and dog fur and disgusting blue lumps of intestine, which looked like sections of frozen hosepipe. The elk had literally torn the dog and the hunter to pieces, goring them with its antlers. In its rage, it had tossed their remains up and hurled them back down on the ground again and again. The moss, rotted vegetation, and branches seemed to have been chewed over by the tracks of a caterpillar tractor. The skis had been reduced to woodchips. All that remained of the gun were its barrels, while of Vitaly himself...

He fetched a spade from the hut, shovelled up what he

could, and buried it on the mound in a shallow grave, having first warmed the earth with a bonfire. He wondered about a cross, but thought better of it. What was the point, when Vitaly believed only in fate.

One time when he was removing the frozen body of a marten from a trap, Vitaly had looked down at the horrifically mutilated little corpse with its angry, glassy, cat-like eyes and said, "Don't take on, mate. You'll have your revenge soon enough." Prophetic words.

Skunk spent the night in Vitaly's hut, loaded up the sledge with food, swept the place very clean, and went back to butcher the elk and sit out the rest of the winter. He broke the forester's rule that dogs should stay outside, and let it in. It curled up under the table, its eyes gleaming, as if just waiting for orders from its new master.

19

Now equipped with all he needed, he could stop worrying about food. The carcass of the elk alone should be enough to keep him and the dog going for a long time. He hibernated like a bear, eating, drinking, seeing vivid daydreams, and losing track of night and day. Indeed, there was now no real day. The sun would break through in the morning somewhere far away, very low, in a billowing tide of pink clouds. Five hundred yards from the hut the scenery no longer emerged from the shadows. For a short time the light broke through, rolling in like dull manganese, trembled on the uneven bank, faded to lilac, and imperceptibly thickened into a suspension of blue-tinged soot. An icy coldness blanketed the expanses with a quilt of impenetrability.

The hush stilled smells, knotted his stomach, and some worrisome embryo sucked away in his entrails. Skunk stopped going outside except very occasionally, when it could not be avoided. He imagined eyes were watching him from every side. Only his sleepy, lethargic husky gave him a degree of brittle confidence that it was just his mind playing tricks.

In the magnificent blackness of the night, the Milky Way hung on skies as hard as a cast mirror, like a fathomless swathe of crusted ice. The moon, stripped bare, virginal, scorched him with her unearthly coldness. Whatever it was that had filled his soul with bubbling, spontaneous merriment had gone, and in its place had settled an unholy trinity of horror, doubt, and the premonition of some incomprehensible and ineluctable misfortune. Skunk felt through the pores of his skin the celestial currents which brought with them infinitesimal prickly particles which were descending on him from remote heights, which had his soul shivering in a blue funk, and bathed everything around in a peculiarly lifeless, dismal music. Dancing like midges, a suspension like pellets of grain filled the air, rattling at the window behind which their life, his and the dog's, had barricaded itself and, turned to ash, was still smouldering under a snowdrift.

Suddenly everything had contracted to this diminutive, muggy space shot through with a mould which you could not shake off. He lay on his bench, listening to the thud, thud, thud of his cardiac muscle; inside him something warm and resilient, but quite clearly apart from him, independent of his will, was pounding away, sometimes faster, sometimes barely even audibly, driving the blood through his heavy, lethargic, engorged limbs. Sometimes he thought back to the gigantic beast from Koloch, standing there in the bushes by the lakeside, huge but with its strength already spent, its eyes sunken, trying to contain the pain in its flank, with its unfeeling rear leg, gazing out through bloody haze at the snowy expanses stretching in the distance. The elk was already a half corpse, it was already half dead, already half-way to being nothing when he, sad little prick that he was, loosed off a bullet and, as if that were not enough, exulted, had been ready to jump for joy at the famous victory which chance had brought his

74

way. What victory? What foe had he vanquished? Crashing down in the bushes, the beast had breathed its last gasp, had taken its leave of all of that it had gazed upon, aloof and brooding, no few times in its life. In just that secretive way, barely poking its nose out of the cover of the trees in order to breathe in the scene of the profoundly dangerous expanse before its feet. Had it been drawn there? Of course, it had come to take its leave, straining every sinew to outpace death. And the bullet? It seemed not even to have noticed it, to have accepted it as its due, and fallen.

And here, now, cut off from the world, Skunk suddenly felt so terribly shamed, felt such pain and fear for the act he had committed; only here, only now did the enormity of his crime come crashing down on him, tormenting and torturing him without let up, without hope of redemption.

When, on top of everything else, a snowstorm was howling outside, and a plank which had torn loose in the attic started to clatter, an answering echo of alarm and misery stole into his heart and he could find no way to escape from it. If only Vitaly had been there... The sound of his own voice seemed alien. He fell silent, and his hearing became extraordinarily sensitive: any creak or scuffling, any tinkling of the aerial wire now threw him into a cold sweat or a fever, and the oil lamp, suddenly deciding to smoke acridly or, on the contrary, to flare up crackling... Was he going out of his mind?

Somebody was paring his spine away, pressing in on his ears, his eyes, jangling a tinny bell inside him. He was out of kilter. The great life-giver, the bringer of peace and tranquillity, had turned away from him.

In a sweat, no longer capable of bringing in firewood, he rolled up in a ball beneath a tangle of blankets, mattresses and pillows in the icy hut, choking from a dry fever in the chill, frosty air. His heart fluttered in his chest when he crawled over to scrape up snow from the doorway and gulp it down with encrusted lips, stinging and bitter, creaking between his teeth, cooling and drying his throat only for an instant. The husky would bound over and lick his face with its rough tongue, but he would drive it away in fear, with a whisper and a ghastly barking cough, and the dog would vanish through the door but soon return, scramble in under the bench and, as if scenting some invisible presence, whine pitifully in fear, thumping its tail on the floorboards and scratching them with its hard, blunt claws.

But whoever had visited this sickness on him also took it from him. On legs of straw Skunk staggered out to the spicy smelling pile of pine logs and, one by one, painfully slowly, stumbling, dragged some in and got the stove going again. He boiled up a salted fish. Scalding his throat, he greedily drank down the evil-smelling broth, slept, woke again, drank some more. No, he did not want to die here. A recalcitrance deeper than fatal indifference healed him.

He had finally glimpsed the face of fear, glanced in sickness beyond a boundary previously inaccessible, and now voraciously, like a vampire, tore the boiled elk meat with his teeth, chewing the rubbery fibres and rejoicing in the warmth spreading to every part of his body. He growled no less voluptuously than the dog over the bones.

The world came back to life, began suddenly and intoxicatingly to smell again. He responded sensuously, with all his heart to the loved, familiar surroundings.

Skunk decided now that it was time to move on, to forget the past. He was drawn again to human company, and supposed that out there everything would fall into place. How, exactly, he made no attempt to anticipate, but just as soon as the days began to grow longer he loaded up the sleigh with provisions and skied off south-west to the land where humans dwelt.

He buried the shotgun and other supplies beneath a rock in a plantation loud with the twittering of sparrows near the railway halt. He had to beat the dog heartlessly with a stick in order to drive it away. He still had some of his own money left, and this had been augmented by two hundred roubles inherited from Vitaly which he had discovered among the hunter's belongings. He bought a third class ticket in order not to attract unwelcome attention by his odd attire. He travelled south into springtime, and his dirty jacket lined with fur became uncomfortably hot. It came in handy as an underlay on the hard carriage bunk.

Part Two

1

"I've screwed my whole life up. I've blown it. I had it all, but that wasn't good enough. I had to go over the top. I could have had the lot, I could gorge myself on chocs and bubbly, but I had to shit all over everything like a stupid, filthy pig, that's what I am, worse than Satan. It was me blew it all, little Danny," his mother wailed, "Me, me, nobody else but me." She hugged Daniil to herself, buried his head in her dressing gown, smothering his face in her hot sagging tits. "Stay with me, Danny. You, at least, treat me right. I'm not some stray she-wolf, I'm your mother, eh? Oh, oh, a she-wolf would be better than me. It's the truth, isn't it? Go on, Danny, say it's the truth!" She ranted on, her lips blue and crusted, and did not let go of him, pinioning his arms, clutching him, trying to hug him some more.

She was drunk, of course. He could smell the acrid smell of cheap sherry a mile away: it hit him as he came in the door.

"You haven't forgotten me, you haven't forgotten your old mother, my little Danny, my son. You've come back to me." She was sitting on the edge of her crumpled bed, a withered woman in a cramped little room. A pair of crutches lay where they had fallen on the floor.

"Forgive me, forgive me for all this mess. I'm really legless now, had a fall, didn't I. Trust me to do something stupid like that."

She was lying as usual, or embellishing reality,

as a large bruise under her eye, her swollen lip, and arms that looked as if they had been pecked by geese unambiguously testified.

"Who did this, Mam?" he asked with a catch in his voice, and hardly recognized himself.

"Oh," she shook her shaggy mop of hair like a mare tormented by a horsefly and gave a sudden smile. Her face lit up, a spark of electricity in her eye. "What does it matter, son?"

"I'll find him..."

"Oh, oh, oh - I've got someone to protect me now. Let me look at you..." She puckered her lips and waved her arms about like a jerky clockwork doll. "How you've grown, my little puppy dog, but just look at me..." And slobbering and spluttering she resumed her lament, scraping her good heel on the floor-boards in an orgy of self-pity. She suddenly switched off the funeral dirge, in a hurry to get out of bed. She straightened her shoulders like a hussar on parade, but ran out of energy before she could get up. There had been enough only to make the gesture, and now she relapsed and her head sank back.

"Take it easy, Mam."

"Okay, okay, whatever you say," she craftily consented, a gleam in her eye, pleased with herself, smugly confident she now had someone to look after her. No sooner had her son gone through to the kitchen to boil some potatoes than she was groping for a bottle in by the wall and gulping it down. Three gulps and it was empty. She started singing an improbably slurred rendition of "Moscow Nights", proclaiming her supreme contentment to the rest of the world.

His mother had never before been so remorseful. To be sure, she had never before been so knocked about either. The neighbours told him the full story later. The police had come and separated her and her latest amour. He was on the verge of taking an axe to her. It was quite an incident. And she said she had slipped and fallen...

He carefully pulled up the blanket, plumped up her pillow, and his mother responded feverishly with a barely coherent, "Oh, sweetheart, oh my sunshine, scamper to me, my little bunny."

He jerked his hand away, deeply upset. He had had enough of her cooing to her sunshines and her little bunnies behind the curtain.

Now that she was warm again and reassured she was either in a muddle or lacked any other terms of endearment and had simply murmured her usual. Already her breathing was coming deep and measured from underneath the blanket, and like a sunken log in a lake her injured foot was sticking out from beneath the blanket, while her split lips were reciting the litany of her marital misfortunes in sleep.

He dived into his cubby hole and pulled the curtain to. He felt the chill of the sheet as he pulled it over his bare chest and he drew his knees up to his chin. The pillow might not be any too clean, but, much slept on, it was his own. The blanket might be on the short side, but he snuggled into its familiar form. And full of happiness, feeling light in the head, he breathed away, fugging up his burrow. He had not enjoyed falling asleep so much for a long time.

2

Things were altogether different, however, when he hit the town. He got absolutely nowhere with the technical college, of course, and had in any case missed a year. His mother managed to persuade the manageress at work to let him on to the gravy train, working at the reception point for old bottles by the bathhouse. Twenty-five, thirty, even fifty roubles a day could stick to your fingers with no problem, and money makes all the difference. His workmates drank the money as fast as they made it, and the teetotal Skunk stuck out like a sore thumb. They ragged and mocked, and then got used to him and left him to do as he pleased. He was a big boy now. And the big boy was beginning to grow whiskers. Not yet a moustache, but fish-like whiskers at the side of his mouth and down on his chin. He bought himself a razor, shaving cream, aftershave, and completed the transformation with a jacket, trainers, and press-stud jeans. "Hey, what a peacock," his mother enthused, when she was in a state to enthuse.

Her broken bone mended and then it was back to the old routine. Her amorous urges had abated not one whit, and once again little Danny was in the way. Except when she needed to bum a few roubles off him for a drink. "It's for my medicine, Danny," she would wheedle then, but any other time... He gave up on her and they lived together like strangers. "You should get yourself a curly headed girlfriend instead of sitting all day in front of the television," which, being translated, meant that she wanted the flat for her own purposes.

Some gigolo would gallantly offer him a drink, but Skunk would pointedly not notice or subject them to a glassy stare, and they would melt away into nothingness because, basically, they were pond life, not men.

But the joys of spring were not to be ignored, and its force no longer to be deflected by schoolboy stratagems; he was treated now to dreams in full colour in his sleep. He tried to resist, scared, to tell the truth, ignorant of the moves in this new game. Girls would eye his clothing with interest. He could feel the tug on the line but... he only went all tense and walked past them looking surly. But then one time he bumped into Zhenka. He thought he had got over her, but no chance. His knees started shaking as if he were an old goat.

"Sku-unk, hell-o! Haven't seen you for a-ges. Where you be-een?"

"Away."

"Where are you now?"

"Bottle unit, recycling bottles."

"Wow, great. Hey, Skunk, want to come to the disco tonight?"

"Okay."

"Great. See you up the hill at seven. Okay?"

She graced him with a smile and even a little wave. Was that a come-on?

He ironed a shirt in the kitchen and almost burned it. His mother rumbled him instantly. "Not going out with a lady friend by any chance?"

"What's it to you?"

"Oh, nothing, nothing," she said, leering carnivorously. This she could understand. This was close to her heart.

He slicked his hair down into a neat parting in front of the mirror, and headed off to the dance floor at Merry Hill. He positioned himself to one side, with his hands behind his back.

"Sku-unk!"

She had seen him. She was here. But not alone: with a gaggle of friends, guys and girls who looked like they dealt in currency.

"Hey, people, this is Danny the Skunk. I told you about him."

They shook hands, moving as circumspectly as hazel grouse on shingle.

"Wanna slug?" His lip curled, but he took it in order not to lose face. He wasn't at the bottle bank now. He downed the vodka for Zhenka, managed not to choke on it, carried it off okay, but as for a repeat: no thanks. His head flushed hot and he stood close to Zhenka, but things did not work out: she had this hunk in attendance. So what had he got so excited for? He decided to slope off quietly, but Zhenka got in first. She brought another girl over when it was a slow dance and said, "Valyusha, you dance with Danny". She introduced them and immediately went back to her guy, having fixed up her friend. That was probably why he had been invited in the first place.

Anger boiled up in him, and his ear lobes prickled, but he sensed an all-too-familiar loneliness in her. He could scent that a mile away, and melted a bit towards this Valyusha. He took her home after the dance, and was even invited up for tea. Her mother kept watch at the church every third day. He went for it unabashed, and they got as far as snogging on the sofa, but at that she called a halt. He took it philosophically: he'd got his foot in the door. She said okay to going to a movie, and stroked his hand when they parted.

Before he fell asleep he tried stroking his hand himself, but it wasn't the same: it didn't leave him gasping.

3

After work he would change out of his workclothes and be off. Five was when Valyusha stopped work in the canteen. They would meet up in the park or go to the video cinema. She couldn't live without the movies. She wasn't too bright. They would be walking through the streets after the film, through the porridgey air of a white summer night, like dogs out for their walk, and she would say, "Really fantastic. Her bra had a butterfly on it. Did you see?" There was no need to reply. She didn't mind. Just nod. The main thing was to keep in step.

"And a tiger-striped swimsuit. I've never seen one like that before."

Valyusha walked this way and that, but always with a tentative come-on: where had all that lack of confidence gone that he had noticed the first day? When the lights went down in the cinema Skunk lost his head, but he wasn't allowed to touch. Valyusha sat bolt upright waiting for her fairy story. After, when they were strolling through the streets, he would get as stiff as a stallion, but no. Keep yourself to yourself! He showed her the old pumping station one time. "Want to go in?" he asked pointedly.

"Oh, lay off, you can't mean it. You're nuts. On a rubbish tip, or what?"

You'd have thought her mother's sad little room with its

threadbare sofa was a palace. Her mother had been brought up in an orphanage in Siberia; her father had been exiled there. He brought them back home with him and promptly died of cancer of the tongue. Valyusha told Skunk about his tongue not fitting in his mouth any more. She was glad to go to work in the canteen after finishing eighth grade at school. Her mother, Aunt Vera to Skunk, didn't try to talk her out of it. She had drudged away in the canteen herself before she got her legs scalded.

Valyusha's mother was a thoroughly decent woman. "Dan-Dan-Danny." Funny how much he liked the way she said that. She made him feel really welcome. She wasn't clever, and had no idea how things stood between them. Or maybe she had. But probably not. What did she still need to do in her life? Get Valyusha fixed up, and Skunk did not smoke or drink. The money in his pockets was not stolen, not at his age; he hadn't been in the army yet. And he had real money. It was beyond her. She had never had that kind of money in her life. "Roses, look at them! They must have set you back a good twenty-five roubles. What sort of nonsense is that?" But he could tell she was pleased.

Valyusha counted up how much he spent on her too. He bought her a watch which played seven different tunes, in a plastic cover with a red strap, two hearts on the dial, and waterproof.

"A hundred roubles?!" she gasped.

One time he brought champagne from the market for fifty roubles. He spent his money as it came in, putting nothing aside. It was not that he didn't enjoy it, but he was up against Zhenka's pals. At the disco they strutted about like pheasants and really did have money to burn. Of course, any time he wanted... but no: he wasn't going to turn them over. He knew what fear was now. Anyway, what did they know about life?

Valyusha danced, and he hated it. It was a real pain with his bandy legs. He could only really manage smooching, and spent most of his time as a wallflower. And why should she get huffy. He didn't like it, he couldn't do it, and he didn't intend to learn. He stood there, listening in the intervals to their one topic of conversation: who had made how much. He noticed Valyusha's ears flapping. These people really knew how to live! Sure they did, until the first time the police pulled them in and then they would spill their guts and shop their own mother and father. That was the kind of friends they were.

At home his mother never laid off. What was going on? Who was he seeing? What was she like?

"Is it that little totty I saw you with at the cinema?"

"Mam!"

"She's rubbish, she is, rubbish. She'll only mess you about."

"Mam, pack it in!" he yelled, seriously upset.

But those two days would drive him crazy. They would all have tea together in the evenings: Aunt Vera making it for him endlessly, sermonizing in a weird, pious tone. It all went in one ear and out the other with him, just as it did with Valyusha. Valyusha had given up on her mother's Bible-bashing long ago. "That's enough, Mum. Go to bed."

And off she would go, and stay firmly out of the way in her own curtained off corner of the room, grunting occasionally, trying to get her scalded legs comfortable. He felt sorry for the poor, stupid old fool. They would sit, the two of them, at the table, Valyusha with her head in the clouds, he waiting. Even when her mother fell asleep Valyusha wouldn't let him get intimate. For heaven's sake, they could have done it on the quiet! Some hope!

As a grey dawn was breaking he would go back home along the river bank, to get in another hour's sleep. The air was nippy. A steamer would be chugging away in the distance. St Andronicus's stone was at the half-way mark, surrounded now by a wooden balustrade. Religion was no longer frowned on. Now people could light their candles without having to look over their shoulders. There was even a procession behind the Cross on holidays. When was it that he had flown on the rock? Had he dreamed it? He looked at the water. It was flat and empty and gleamed in by the banks. Inside him his heart was empty too.

At home everyone had fallen asleep for a hundred years. His mother was snoring with a high whistle: her man of the moment was sprawled out and also snoring, but throatily. Cigarette ends, dried out tinned food, stale bread, a gnawed piece of gristle lay on the floor. He threw himself into his section of the room, pulled the curtain to, and was lost to the world. In next to no time the alarm clock was hammering needles into his head: up time! Valyusha had to get up in the morning too, and return to her steaming kitchens to heave great bubbling urns of barley coffee and break eggs into the spitting fat and make breakfast for the dear tourists.

At work only the ribbing of his mates brought him round.

"Get your leg over then?"

"Uhuh!"

"Look, guys, our randy little colt has got a taste for oats. Off you go, get yourself a bit of kip."

The little colt really had got a taste for oats. He was as randy as hell. Everything came together in an agony of anticipation. He had ants in his pants and could think of nothing else. He wanted to get his rocks off, desperately, and nothing else mattered.

4

He was used to reining in his desires, but he found it impossible to humour Valyusha all the time. Increasingly he let her chatter wash over him, and only shrugged in puzzlement if she got offended by his aloofness. After all, he needed a bit of understanding too, and his need seemed perfectly natural and straightforward: but Valyusha was incapable of compromising her established routine. She liked being with people, while

Skunk found they got on his nerves as much as ever. Nobody nowadays was going to shout all round the neighbourhood, "Wonky legs, wonky legs!" but the memory still haunted him: he had only to plunge again into a crowd for the guardedness he seemed to have grown out of in the forest to come welling up again from the pit of his stomach. He was constantly on the alert, waiting for the attack to come, anticipating it. Those indomitable, flaring nostrils of his were alive to the scent of danger in the alien air of their dishonestly ordered world. He wanted continuity and peace, while Valyusha found this phoney, grasping life suited her down to the ground.

May came. Now the dance floor was open not merely on Mondays and Thursdays but every day of the week, and Valyusha, gazing at him imploringly, would now regularly drag him up there, overriding even her passion for the movies. Scrupulously disguising his irritation as weary indifference, he would take her on to the floor, granting her permission to have fun with a nod of his head, before sloping off into the shadows, away from the flashing of the disco lights, and look meditatively over the heads of the crowd, waiting for her to get fed up, remember about him, and come running back. She did come running back, too, but always with the same refrain, "Danny, let's go. It's great. You'll soon learn!"

"No, I can't be bothered." He tried to modulate his tone, but it always sounded wry, almost rude.

"Oh, you. Well I'll go. That okay?"

Skunk's brooding restraint and strangeness gave him a certain authority at the dance floor. He was accepted for what he was and nobody tried either to rib him or push their friendship on him. They shook hands with him when they met with ritual respect. They didn't simply give him five, but took his hand properly, holding it firmly and releasing it lingeringly, and then he would retire to his isolation, just as Moose used to in the square in front of the school, in a sense present, but in another sense not, noticeable for his independence and for his steady awareness of his right as a free man to stand there in just that manner.

Valyusha was undoubtedly taken by the special status of her escort. On more than one occasion Skunk intercepted glances furtively cast his way. The other lads were obviously talking about him, but when he tried to find out what they were saying Valyusha always avoided answering him, and instead demurely lowered her eyes in an expression of dog-like devotion and admiration. At the same time, however, she began to behave quite inexplicably. More and more often all that dragonfly lightness of hers would vanish. She would seem somehow crushed, fall silent, and lose her prettiness even as he watched, like a snowman in the yard who, a moment ago, had been sparkling in the sunlight and now was cast in cold shadow. His attempts to get to the root of the problem usually led to a quarrel verging on hysterics; or even worse, Valyusha would put on a hammy act and try to register radiant happiness.

This would be followed by a wall of silence which he was powerless to break down. Like an illness, this far from random breakdown of communication undermined and weakened his power which, until recently, had been undisputed. He became anxious and very, very angry. Skunk was horrified to catch himself sometimes feeling like punching her in the face, really beating her up, so enraging did he find Valyusha's bouts of sullenness.

When he went home his mother poured oil on the fire, impertinently quizzing him and sometimes openly deriding him: "Didn't let you have it again?"

He had difficulty holding himself back from clouting her, and retreated to his corner blacker than a thundercloud.

5

Fate delivered him a gift which exceeded all his expectations. He had finished work as usual, popped home to change and grab a bit to eat, and gone out to the park. Aunt Vera would be guarding the church today, and he was expecting to stay over with Valyusha. But for the first time since they had met, Valyusha did not appear. Having waited an hour and more, he almost ran to her house with a presentiment of disaster. God only knows what misfortunes he imagined. For some reason he decided that something really dreadful must have happened to Aunt Vera.

For a long time there was no response to his ringing, but Skunk's ear detected movement. Someone was in the flat. He gave the door a good kicking, and heard Valyusha's familiar steps coming to open it.

She did open it, but did not let him in. Instead she squeezed herself through a narrow opening and came out on to the landing. A hardness and coldness he had not met before did not frighten him off. He tried to put his arms round her, but she moved away.

"You know what, just piss off, will you? I've had it up to here with you, get it?" she muttered without further preliminaries and with unambiguous loathing in her voice.

"What's got into you?" he asked, no longer trying to move in on her, but looking her straight in the eyes.

Valyusha did not look away as usual, and when she spoke the words came tumbling out, harsh, edgy, but final:

"I'm pissed off with you. Is it really so difficult to understand? You're really weird, a right pain in the arse, everybody says so. You're the only person who thinks you're something special. The others have driven me round the bend asking when I'm going to dump you. I stuck it out because I thought you would get the message. You only... Go away, Skunk. Just do me a favour. I made my mind up ages ago. I never did love you, I'm telling you straight... You are like a wild animal, you only want one thing, you... Go away. Don't torture me."

She finally broke down and burst into tears.

"Valyusha, what's wrong with you?" He tried to come

near her again, but she screamed, "Go away, go away, if you know what's good for you. I'm not on my own. I've got a new boyfriend. We met at the hotel. He'll beat the shit out of you. Now do you understand?"

She tried to bar the door with her body, but Skunk pushed her aside and burst into the apartment. A well-built, modishly dressed man of between twenty-five and twenty-seven was standing in the corridor. He stood his ground, with his hands behind his head in a relaxed pose.

"Something still not clear? Want me to make it a bit clearer?" He did not come at him. Confident of his superiority, he merely flexed his biceps demonstratively, as if stretching, straightened his massive arms out, and again folded them behind his head.

Skunk did not stop to think. Already fully aware of the situation, he did not see just walking away as an option and rushed at him, aiming his head at the man's solar plexus, but running straight into a fist instead. His adversary was well trained and, without giving him time to come to his senses, booted him hard in the groin and twisted his arm behind his back. He led his doubled up victim out on to the landing, planted a boot in his back, and sent him flying. Skunk counted the stairs with his ribs before slamming into a wall and slithering along it. The pain in his groin prevented him from straightening up, or even breathing in.

The door shut behind him and stayed shut. Skunk heard Valyusha shrieking hysterically, unrestrainedly, and the booming bass of her musclebound moron trying to calm her down.

He unbuckled with difficulty and went downstairs, leaning heavily on the bannisters.

She had sold herself to the highest bidder then, the silly cow.

He sat in the park until late into the night, the pain gradually subsiding. Thank God, the silly prick hadn't damaged his tackle. He had got him in the abdomen. Skunk swallowed blood and waited for his gums to stop bleeding. He rubbed his two bumps. Finally, coping with the pain, he limped his way home. First he needed to have a good night's sleep. Tomorrow was Victory Day. Then he would see.

6

In the morning the aching had subsided. It was only the bruise on his cheek that still harrowed him like a fresh slap and burned him inside.

Was it really only the money? Well, that was easy to check out. He left the house and sloped through the streets for a long time in search of prey. His body tensed, tingling in anticipation. Doubts and scruples evaporated instantly and he again felt the familiar, delectable excitement of the chase coursing through his veins.

There weren't many punters around, and those there were were neatly dressed and, for the most part, with children in tow and therefore with no money, pointlessly shambling the holiday away. There were a few drunks around too, mostly concentrated in courtyards, but there was nothing to take off them. He needed a high-stepping wheeler-dealer, but that kind were not awake yet. Their element was twilight, after dark, the restaurants.

So he went in to the old Slavno cemetery, which was bustling because of the holiday. What sort of person would let a spring day pass without paying a visit to the family graves? An endless file of old women was flowing through the gates. They were wearing headscarves and heavy jackets, still in their winter felt boots with galoshes over them, unimaginable clothes someone had passed on to them, some with a bucket, some with a bag with a bread roll, an egg, a handful of millet for the sparrows, and a grimy three-rouble note: their last, earmarked for a candle or for greasing the palm of the cemetery attendant. Today was their day.

Skunk sat down for a moment on a bench beside a well tended grave, a special seat for any passing by, solidly carpentered, freshly painted not long before at Easter, with a little table and an empty drinking glass on its special shelf for drinking to the memory of the dead, which it would be a sin to remove or steal, and which it was blessed to use and drink from. In a depressing, grey crowd shuffling along the sandy path, their sticks tapping, exchanging the same predictable remarks they had exchanged a hundred times before, the old women were creeping along all in the same direction, clearly with some end in view, unhurriedly, one behind the other until you saw spots before your eyes. Inquisitive, Skunk made tracks to follow them to some destination behind a mound, beyond the old church which had been closed down, possibly to the war memorial with its standard issue plaster soldier. Most likely that was it.

But then a taxi rolled up to the gate. A scrawny, pock-marked old bird with a beak-like nose and a limp hopped out, hastily opened the door, and there emerged into the light a sturdy, red-cheeked fellow with a neatly trimmed beard and cropped hair wearing a sweater and a kind of grey windcheater, and carrying a small briefcase. The old women slowed down, turned their faces towards the new arrival, and started smiling and bowing.

"The Father has arrived, the Father is here!" word rustled down the sidepaths.

The reverend Father had meanwhile undone his artificial leather briefcase in a businesslike manner, extracted a rolled up cassock, pulled it over his head, hung a bronze cross on his chest, handed his accompanying churchwarden a censer and the briefcase, and strode into the cemetery, not forgetting to cross himself before passing through the gates. The old women clustered round him and started fussing, trying to kiss his hand and asking his blessing, but the priest made a gesture as if brushing them off himself, and said something fierce above their heads. They immediately made way and then scurried after him. The burly priest was already striding on ahead, and disappeared round the hill.

Out of idle curiosity Skunk tagged along, not joining the mainstream, but following a little parallel sidepath. He was in the shadow of spreading trees, hidden out of sight of the crowd drawn up on the patch of land around the memorial. An amazing number of people had come, several hundred at least, and those who could not find a place thronged the paths around, between the grave palings, shifting from one foot to the other as they waited for the service to begin.

The priest turned to face the memorial, a plaster warrior with misshapen eyes, lists of names of those at rest in the communal grave, the lettering eroded by the rains and snow, carved on keeling concrete headstones. In his left hand he held a small book with a velvet bookmark, and he raised his other hand a little towards heaven, as if concentrating his mind, but in fact waiting for his attendant lady sexton to get the incense burning in the censer. When at last the incense was lit, the woman swung the censer aloft like a sling with an expression of brutality on her face and presented it, billowing spicy fumes, to the priest. The great liturgical prayer of the *ekteniya* began.

"In peace we pray to the Lord."

The priest's voice was not particularly thunderous, but silence fell instantly. Everybody crossed their foreheads, and all that could be heard was the rustling of paper. Those who had not already done so were passing over the heads of those standing in front notes of intercession for the dead. More to the point, these were accompanied on their voyage by banknotes: crumpled one rouble, three rouble, occasionally five rouble notes, and even one or two red tenners. This veritable ocean of paper funnelled its way to the sexton. The slips of paper were pushed into her hands by two old women standing specially behind her. They unfolded the notes for her, and the priest's unofficial deputy managed somehow both to sing and keep an eye on the censer, taking it from him now and again to add more of the resin, and prodding him in the back to pass him another pile of slips bearing names.

On the memorial's headstones candles were burning. A few of the worshippers tried falteringly to join in the responses. The priest himself only very occasionally gave voice:

"For the remission of sins of the departed in the sure and certain hope of resurrection we pray to the Lord."

While the choir responded, the priest read out the names or, more precisely, mumbled them like so much mumbo-jumbo at top speed in order to get through them all. He galloped through, barely pausing for breath. But still the stream of paper did not dry up. His assistant was plainly wearying as she continued to bend down to the briefcase on the ground, shoving more and more piles of roubles into it.

Skunk was standing on a slight hill, hearing everything, seeing everything. The briefcase's voracious gullet was constantly re-filled as the priest's cascading words, hurried, almost hasty, seemed to have established a rhythm which was sucking more and more money out of the pockets of his congregation.

The priest continued endlessly to throw out into the hush of the windless cemetery the names of the slain, of those who had died of natural causes long ago or not so long ago, of the martyred, relatives and friends, the dearly loved and the not so dearly loved but interceded for in the solemnity of the moment, after something had touched a heart string.

And then, when all the lists seemed finally to have been read, the priest immediately returned the slips of paper he had processed, not looking down at them, and they were reverently received back as something of worth, and pressed to bosoms. The time was approaching for the general intercession for the dead. Strange as it might seem, Skunk remembered this service. Back in his childhood with his grandmother, his young mind had effortlessly memorized the words, and now he knew that the ritual was nearly at an end. He began to listen carefully, turning his head to catch the sound, and ceasing for the time being to concern himself with the briefcase.

"The most holy patriarchs, the sainted metropolitans, archbishops and bishops, and also those who serve Thee in priestly and monastic orders, the creators of this holy temple, our Orthodox forefathers, fathers, brothers, sisters of mercy who laid down their lives in the war for their Orthodox faith and Fatherland; the faithful slain in fratricidal strife, drowned, burned, rent asunder by wild beasts, those suddenly deceased without absolution, without time to be reconciled with the Church and with their enemies; those slain by their own hand while their mind was disturbed; those for whom we have been asked to pray; those who have nobody to pray for them; and the faithful denied Christian burial; and give them lodging, Lord, in the realms of light and bliss and peace, where there is neither disease nor sorrow nor suffering of the spirit. As the God of mercy who loves the world, forgive them all their transgressions whether of word or deed or wanton thought; for no man can live and not sin, since Thou alone art without sin and Thy justice is justice eternal and Thy word is truth. For Thou art the resurrection and the life and the peace of Thy slaves who have departed this life, oh Christ our God, and to Thee we raise our voices in praise, God the Father Unbegotten, God the Son, and God the Blessed, Life-giving and Most Holy Spirit, now and forever and for time everlasting."

"Amen," the rows of worshippers sighed, before beginning to straighten up and stir their numb legs, and cross their foreheads some more as they bowed to the memorial, the priest's back, and each other. Then they reached out towards the Cross, and there was no denying their longing, but the priest was now clearly in a hurry. The sexton was doing up the briefcase, energetically ramming her fist down on all the money which had been thrown in to it. Then she stood for a while clutching it to her breast, the priest's pickings, answering questions, turning down requests: they were probably being urged to visit individual graves. The priest was having none of it, and again raised his hands heavenwards asking to be allowed through, bowing to all, and heading rapidly for the exit. His smile was tight-lipped, and he physically moved the most obdurate out of the way.

"No, no, I really can't," Skunk heard him say.

"He needs to rest. He has another service to hold today. Be reasonable!" the sexton flared up in exasperation, and wielding the briefcase in one hand and the defunct censer in the other, she marched confidently forward, forcing them back. Their retreat was like a getaway. The priest did not even take off his cassock, but pressed on down the path at an ever-increasing pace, and the old ladies fell behind and began to disperse through the cemetery, to their own special places, and by the time he had reached the entrance gates only three or four had kept up; not in order to make requests, but simply because they wanted to see him off properly and bow one last time.

Skunk had everything worked out. He was standing outside the wall behind a stone pillar, and the instant the sexton came level with him he slapped her hard in the face, wrenched the briefcase out of her hand, rushed over the road, and disappeared into the undergrowth. He went to ground in his pumping station, and in the semi-darkness of the basement, even more filthy and untidy after his long absence, counted the proceeds: eight hundred and thirty-one roubles, a respectable amount even by the standards of the dance floor gigolos. Valyusha would surely rise to this bait, or... He started smoothing out the notes and tying them up in bundles of a hundred with some string he found. He ended up with a good fat wad; untied them again and threw them up in the air like leaves. He delved his hands in them, but no longer got a kick out of it. He again gathered his riches together, sorted them, stashed them away in the hiding place, shoved the empty briefcase behind a pile of rubbish in the corner and, stepping coolly and confidently, went back outside.

7

The next day Skunk glanced without more ado into his hiding place, pulled out the money and stuffed it in his pockets. The bulging jacket made him feel good. He headed for the canteen, knowing that breakfast would be over by now and Valyusha would have a short break when they could talk. He went in up the back staircase and asked a woman in a greasy white coat where he could find Valentina.

"Meat section. You'll find them all in there having a coffee break, the idle layabouts." The woman gestured vaguely down the corridor, and he found his own way, taking care where he put his feet in order not to slip and land in the sticky dirt much traversed by trolley wheels.

In the meat section four women of a certain age were sitting at a large metal-covered table on which a precarious space had been cleared of scraps of meat and bone. Their faces were flushed and sweaty, and they were wearing starched white headscarves, down-at-heel shoes, and dirty, scuffed white coats over their balloon-like breasts and cushion-like bellies. They were in that blissfully switched off state of mind bestowed by a brief respite from backbreaking toil, and were being entertained by a fat boy, his crafty face plainly that of a butcher, in a blood-stained jacket and apron. The boy was spinning them some tale and the women were pretending not really to listen, where in fact they were all ears, empathizing and chuckling or sighing in all the right places, and in all the wrong places too. At the same time they were drinking coffee and eating buns from their own bakery and taking turns to dip a sticky spoon into a large metal pail with gooey jam the colour of axle grease, spreading it generously on a bun, and biting off a good half in one go, before washing it down with evil-looking barley coffee, all the time guffawing and waving away the persistent flies which had yet to find somewhere to land on the ubiquitous but overcrowded flypapers.

"Who are you looking for?" the butcher asked in mid-flight. The women were immediately quiet and gawped at the newcomer with unconcealed idiotic interest.

"Valentina."

"You want the director's office on the left. She's busy tidying up."

For some reason this announcement provoked a great deal of giggling, as if he had said something manifestly indecent. Skunk nodded and went past them, attracting a low whistle as he did so. They evidently approved of his attire.

"That her guy, then?"

"Ask me another. She's got them queueing up, the little filly. What it is to be young," the oldest and heaviest of the women drawled lazily.

Skunk went into the director's panelled office. It boasted a telephone, an armchair, a tall steel safe, and smoked oak-style chairs with red upholstery. Valentina was sitting with her back to him inspecting the finish of her eyelids in the mirror of her powder compact. He closed the door. She caught sight of him in her mirror, turned round abruptly, and equally abruptly looked down at the floor. He had cut off her line of retreat.

"Are we going to talk?" he asked unthreateningly, but it came out very coldly. As it was supposed to. No sentimentality.

"What more is there to talk about, Skunky? I've said all I have to say to you."

"No you haven't. Say it again."

"Danny, don't you understand? I didn't mean you to get hurt. I'm sorry. I really didn't want that, but if you don't go away now I shall scream."

"Wait..."

"What for? Are you deaf? I can't put it any more simply: get lost! You are a complete loner, you are like a bear. You just want to go off and lie in your den sucking your paw, but I'm young and pretty. I am pretty, right? I don't enjoy myself unless I'm with people, I just don't. Understand? Go away,

Skunk, for heaven's sake. I know how you feel, but we're through. You won't get anywhere with me. You're history. And anyway, what could you give me? A life like my mother's? Do you think I'm going to stay in this dump forever? I'm an exile here, an exile, can't you see? Making coffee, mincing meat for meatballs, guzzling jam: call that a life? Oh, how could you understand. It's all the same to you how I feel here. You never even asked. But there's a different world out there. People have fun, they have a life. Do you know what that is? A life!"

"If I didn't give you enough, then here, take this." He began feverishly emptying his pockets, throwing down the wads of money on to the director's shiny table.

"Take it. Take the lot! You need more, I'll bring more. It's child's play."

"This... Where did you get this? Where's it come from? Oh, I know. You've stolen it. How else would you have got it?" The money had thrown her, but only for a minute. She shook her head, and rounded on him with new force. "Well? And what am I supposed to do with it? You think I want to end up in prison, or sit biting my lips waiting for you to get out? No, thank you very much. I'm going to find myself a rich man, but one who doesn't get sent to prison. I want to have a life, a real life, all right?"

She was shouting now, sweeping the money up off the table and, her face contorted with loathing for him, started stuffing it back into his pockets, back where it had come from. He caught her anyway, pressed her to his chest, squeezing her, and for a moment she pressed against him too, but only to regain her balance. She suddenly pushed him away, punched him hard in the face and in an instant was transfigured into a witch. She went for him, trying to scratch his eyes out with her brightly varnished finger nails, shrieking in a frenzy.

Skunk staggered back, fending her off, automatically retreating, now really frightened. He held back his revulsion with difficulty, slipped out through the door and from there slammed it hard in Valyusha's face, knocking her off her feet, and locking it from the outside.

He was shaking. Paying not the least attention to the heads popping out from all over the place, he walked briskly down the corridor pursued by blood-curdling, animal shrieks. Valyusha was hurling herself against the door, yelling in the intervals, "I want a life! I want a life!"

He fled from this madhouse where heavy vapours billowed out of cracks and the smell of rotting vegetables hung in the air, away from their greasy, food-spattered linoleum. He fled as fast as his legs could carry him. Only when he reached the river bank, in a familiar clump of bushes where he had once lit a campfire, did he recover his breath a little and threw himself down in the grass.

8

At first he could not understand, and did not want to know, where he was or why. In some remote recess of his brain the information settled that he was by the river, but he only pressed his face into his hands and himself deeper into grass much trampled by the small boys who came swimming here during the day. He lay there for a long time, until the cold from the soil had gone right through him, and then crawled out from the bushes, out of the damp shade to where the sun baked the bald top of a hillock. He turned over now on to his back, put his hands behind his head, and gazed up mindlessly and silently at the blue sky. Somewhere down below, by the river, children were shrieking and splashing about, the motors of boats puttered and whined, but he lay so as to see nothing except the sky: neither the water, nor the city. He kicked off his trainers and presented his wrinkled, sweaty feet to the breeze. The sun warmed and burned him and he screwed up his eyes in the heat and bright sunlight, following through

100

narrow slits the way the clouds sculpted themselves, forming weird figures as they drew themselves up to full height, tall, grey and substantial.

He had long been aware of the calming effect lines had on him: not just any line, not straight or nervous lines, the more they flowed and billowed the better, the more restfully his eye took them in.

What a lovely figure Valyusha had when she was feeling amorous, lying on the sofa, motionless and at peace, and what an agglomeration of broken, sharp angles she had been today with her flailing arms, her twitching eye, her lips drawn in a thin, straight sneer when she was breaking away from him, setting about him, driving him away.

He suddenly remembered that girl in the village with the house he had stolen the shotgun from. He remembered the whole scene: her tying her father's tie, her little brother running riot, and how it had all suddenly vanished when she came out in her grown-up dress, completely altered, slightly wooden, with her stiff-looking father in his stupid jacket.

Skunk pulled a blade of grass, chewed it for a while, and then spat it out together with the light green saliva which tasted slightly bitter, but pleasant. The boys in grandmother's village had told hair-raising tales about the liver sucker which lived in the roots of grass and could get into your stomach as quick as a flash and soften your liver and destroy it and you died in agony. Then he had pictured it, not as a germ with no legs, but as something with a body, slimy, a kind of snail with the legs of an earwig. He had been scared, and held his breath, and looked very carefully at the blade of grass, but had still put it in his mouth and sucked its sap, live, astringent, fresh, the taste lingering on his tongue. Remembering how scared he had been then, he sniggered now and pulled another blade, plump sedge grass this time, put it in his mouth carefully in order not to cut his lips, and chewed it to a mush, the fibres which had not been completely broken down themselves seeming to nibble at his tongue and cheeks as stubbornly at a bullock down by the river in the evening.

And like that bullock, he felt an urge from time to time to bellow, to draw the sound out with his lower lip, but he repressed the urge and contented himself with a toss of his head. Life must go on. Good luck to Valyusha in her seeking. "Live your life, my little sunshine, live your life," his grandmother had sometimes said to him, smoothing his hair, and her old chapped hands had been amazingly soft...

From his grandmother his thoughts jumped to the old grannies at the cemetery: he remembered the line of them, the endless shuffling of their shoes along the path, the deep voice of the priest, and the rustling of the slips of paper with the names. The money in his pockets immediately reminded him of its presence, pressing into him. What use was it all to him now? Again a sense of emptiness descended on him, like the evening which was now stealing over the earth. Cold air, heavy with dew, was wafting up from the river, but he lay there some time yet before rousing himself, brushing off the grass which had stuck to him, rubbing a cheek which had gone to sleep, and wandering on his way. In this frame of mind, aimless and carefree, he strolled along till he found himself at St Andronicus's stone. He stood for a while by the balustrade, frowning vacantly at the lump of rock which the lips of generations of devout women had kissed to a shiny smoothness, the melted candle ends, and the icon lamp which now burned in a metal lantern. He spat on the ground and slowly climbed the stairs tread by creaking tread, not turning round to look at the city on the far side of the river, up and up, and childishly shoved his thumb into his downturned mouth.

Up there it was only a couple of yards along the tarmac path to the church. He went to the gate, counting the beggar pigeons which were settling themselves for the night on the cornices.

"Danny!"

He jumped, but immediately took himself in hand and turned round, his face set in its now habitual detached expression, dark eyes looking out from under his brows.

"Danny!"

Aunt Vera was hobbling across the square heading straight for him with arms outstretched. Before he could utter a word, she fell upon his breast, put her arms round him, and gave him a great hug, a diminutive woman in a clean, much washed headscarf and an old, worn out man's overcoat.

"Danny! What has she done, may God forgive her, Danny! She has driven you away, you wonderful boy, and now the silly fool is howling. I say to her, where's Danny? And she jumps up and goes for me, Danny. She's never screamed at me like that before, never, and stamping her feet like a nanny goat and she's all for grabbing me by the hair. And then that jaw-breaker turns up, her boxer. Well, you know all about him, I know, the neighbour told me everything. I just ran out. She drove me out herself. Off you go, she says, go guard your church. Well, off I did go, Danny, thinking about you all the way here, thinking, and now look, the Lord has sent you to me. You have to forgive me, dear Danny, that hussy has been snared by the Devil, the horned villain, you must forgive me for what she's done."

"Aunt Vera, stop, calm down, calm down..." But she was gripping him as firmly as a keening mourner clutches the corner of a coffin and had no intention of letting go.

"You have come to church, to church, haven't you, Danny?" She looked at him with such hope and joy that he suddenly lied to her with a sense of relief.

"Yes, Aunt Vera, I've come to church."

"That's wonderful, Danny, that's so good. Let us go in, let us go in. I'll open up for you, and make you a nice cup of tea. Soften your heart, let the pain all come out, don't bottle up the bad things. That butterfly of mine doesn't deserve you.

Sinner that I am, I can tell you that. You don't bear her any grudge, in your heart, eh Danny?"

She really was glad to have met him, but was also plainly frightened and anxious to deflect his anger from her daughter.

"Come on, am I really that scary? Pack it in, Aunt Vera. What grudge? Let her get on with living her life."

"Well, thank God, thank God for that, Danny. Now there's no way I shall let you go. Come on in with me, you dear boy, you can help me with my work."

She raised a finger to her lips. "Shhh! The restorer will be here soon. He is going to be working through the night. We have to take the icon down for him, and it's a very heavy one. The Last Judgement. Father, forgive us, for we know not what we do."

He could not refuse, and in any case had no wish to. He walked in front, and Aunt Vera tripped along behind, rattling away as if the words were sunflower seeds she was cracking, mindless things she always said, but Skunk was not listening. He advanced heavily over the sandstone slabs with which, in time for last Easter, they had paved the church yard.

9

It was shadowy and warm inside the church, especially after coming in from the raw evening. Everything was scrubbed clean and the well swept and beaten mats and rugs smelled of cooling incense, warm wax, and something else besides: human breath, perhaps, but not the stale, suffocating sweaty atmosphere of church holidays, just a lingering physical warmth. From the depths of the church, as present as the gentle darkness, barely touched by the light of the green icon lamps, large eyes looked out, the first thing to attract his gaze; the scale-like gilding on the faces of the saints glinted and, already sensitized, he began to make out figures emerging from pillars, hovering on walls, materializing on the interior of the great central dome which lived a separate life of its own.

Aunt Vera clicked a switch and dim electric light came on from bulbs dispersed throughout the body of the church. They did not cheer the place up, merely enlivened its expanses a little, chasing shadows away into the corners, caressing, clinging to the gilt of the elaborate merchant's iconostasis with its heavy bunches of grapes, wing-like scrolls and vignettes which encompassed the praying Virgin with her sad, meditative, almond-shaped eyes drawn towards the central crucifix.

Aunt Vera promptly got down on her knees, bowed three times and crossed her forehead before thumping it down on the scrubbed stone floor. Skunk was standing behind her. Involuntarily, mechanically, in a gesture ingrained since childhood, three fingers of his right hand came together and travelled from brow to belly, and thence to each shoulder blade.

"Danny, Danny," Aunt Vera had noticed. "My dear boy, get down on your knees. Christ who redeems our sins will forgive everything and bring peace to your soul." Her eyes immediately filled with tears of emotion, but seeing Skunk freeze and put his arms straight down at his sides, waiting unspeaking for her to finish, she curbed her ardour, whispered something over the flagstones, made several more quick crosses as if darning a hole with a needle in order to drive away any merrily squealing imps which were sure to be riding in on the draught, got up and went out into the half-light of the side chapel, beckoning him to follow.

Skunk went after her, trying to fight off a strange torpor, as if his body had been pumped full of drugs. The feeling lasted only a few moments, and then Aunt Vera's reedy voice called him, affectionate as usual, but with a hint of lamentation. "Danny, Danny, come here and give an old lady a hand, my dear." There by the entrance, its face leaning towards the wall, stood a huge icon the size of the church door, painted across five boards and held by three roughly hewn crosspieces.

"There, there it is, may God forgive and have mercy on

us. The Last Judgement of Christ. We need to take hold of it and get it up on to the trestle so that everything is ready when he comes. He will start work as soon as he gets here. He promised to have it finished by tomorrow. He's young, just like you, Danny, but a real craftsman. During the day he works on the scaffolding cleaning the walls, and at night he works here, may the Lord save and protect him."

Only then did Skunk notice that scaffolding had been erected on the walls of the side chapel right up to the drum of the dome. Dustsheets were draped there, and jars and pots of paint were ranged in the corner. Little bottles of turpentine and housepainter's and artist's brushes were steeping in buckets.

"There's a team of workmen during the day, but this one, Seryozha, gets a couple of hours' sleep and he's back for the night to earn a bit extra. He was born in Stargorod, but he has his job in Moscow. That's where he studied, Danny, so that's where he lives now; and he comes back to us for the summer by agreement with the Diocese."

Aunt Vera pulled a large trestle out of the corner, placed a standard lamp alongside, and moved over out of the darkness a table with the restorer's bits and pieces.

"Well, God give us strength, take your time. Little by little we'll heave it up there. It weighs a ton, but there we are."

Skunk looked round, measured his strength against the task, and moving Aunt Vera aside, took hold of the icon, and lifted it with a snatch off the ground. With much anxious commentary and sighing but without the slightest mishap, the panel was finally placed on the trestle. It was large and broad, with a wide prominent border, and covered with a layer of greenish black soot. Only here and there were there white patches which looked as though they had been filled in with plaster, and at the top, restored to its original ochre hue, a strip had been cleaned which bore the head inscription: "The Second Coming of Christ in Glory".

For some reason Aunt Vera immediately started snivelling

and pressed her lips to the blackened surface, crossing herself and, shifting in agitation from one foot to the other, whispered, "There, Danny, look, that's the sinners in Hell: some of them are having to lick red hot frying pans, and some are nailed to a spade and being put in an oven; some of them are being lashed mercilessly with scourges. Oh, such a gnashing of teeth, I am afraid to look. I know what's waiting there for us sinners."

Skunk found her childish fears comical: "Come off it, Aunt Vera, you'll fly straight up into heaven..." but he stopped abruptly, so severe was the look she gave him. He had no idea she could look so serious.

"How am I ever going to get to heaven, Danny? Heaven is where the righteous go, but we sinners... Oh, don't talk nonsense, you foolish boy, don't talk about it. Let us rather go and put the tea on. Seryozha will be here soon. I'll have the tea ready for him, and he'll need boiling water for his work. We've been talking far too much," she said with obvious relief at leaving a taboo and frightening topic, and slipped ever so quietly down to the crypt, to the baptistry where the gas ring stayed and the kettle, and the obligatory dried bread rings, sweets and sugar for the tea, and already stale communion bread left over from the morning that crunched when you bit it.

The kettle was soon boiling. The bell at the door promptly rang and the icon restorer made his appearance, still young, with moderately long hair and a bag slung over his shoulder. He was wearing jeans and sneakers better suited to summer, dragged one leg slightly, and his cheerfulness instantly banished the sense of spookiness Aunt Vera had created.

"What, have you been getting in a state again, Aunt Vera?" he asked, still at the door.

"Don't talk about it, Seryozha. Danny and I were scared out of our wits while we were moving it. The church is completely empty. I got goosebumps all over me."

"It's going to get worse: just you wait till I've cleaned it off and you see it in full colour!"

"Oh, my sins, my sins. I shan't go to look at it. I'd do better to stay right here and pray."

They drank the tea and Seryozha prepared to go back upstairs. Skunk was intrigued and, overcoming his timidity, he asked, "Need any help? Maybe I can fetch things for you or something?"

"If you're bored here, let's go. I'll get you washing off. It can only save me time."

Aunt Vera said something as they were leaving, but they were no longer listening. Seryozha climbed confidently up the steep staircase built into the church wall, chuckling and apparently talking to himself:

"The Last Judgement frightens the silly old biddy. She really is from darkest Siberia. Just wait. She won't stick it out. She'll creep out towards midnight. Anyway, why does she guard the church if it scares her?"

They went over to the trestle. Seryozha laid out on the table the tools of his trade: scalpels, dentist's hooks, palette knives, tiny scissors, and quickly dashed a purple solution from a bottle into a jar adding, or perhaps not adding, something to it, shook it around, and examined it against the light.

"Methylated spirits is something else! Some brainy Jew thought it up and, incidentally, got himself a Stalin prize into the bargain. The process is irreversible. It's so simple: you mix ink pencil, some paraffin, some spirit, and you don't need to refine it. It's the best medicine for a stomach ulcer: tans it and dries it up all at the same time. Want some to warm you up?"

"I don't think so. Thanks anyway."

"Suit yourself. I'm going to down a dram. It's so damned cold." He poured some out of the bottle into a glass, took a gulp of water, held it in his mouth and then, without grimacing, took the purple decoction, and again gulped down some water. "A chaser, just for luck!"

Then he carefully unwrapped a sweet, put it under his tongue and sucked it as happily as a baby. Humming something to himself, he started winding a wad of cotton wool on to a stick.

"Right then, this is what you do," he said, showing Skunk how. "You start from the right and I'll start from the left. You dip it in the meths and put it straight on the grunge. Then you rub the muck like mad, and don't go easy on the cotton wool. When that wad gets dirty, wind yourself a new one."

Having demonstrated, he set to work on the surface without more ado, looking over now and again to see how Skunk was getting on, giving him more advice occasionally like, "Don't press too hard or you'll lift all the gilding off. Gently does it, that's the way. The dirt will come off of its own accord."

Sure enough, the spirit did wash the soot off splendidly. The grime of centuries soaked it up like a sponge and softened as you watched, behaved just as it was supposed to, and came away from the panel entirely on to the cotton wool.

"Now we'll cheer it up in no time at all. You think I want to spend all night on it? No way. We'll give it a quick once over and it will be as good as new. Then we'll just go over it again, restore the eyes and wings, give them back their haloes, varnish the panel, and that will be that. Priests don't care what it looks like just as long as it gleams."

Skunk was half-listening to him, and was astonished by the contrast between the reactions of Aunt Vera and this restorer, who seemed to believe neither in God nor the Devil, in spite of the cross he had dangling round his neck.

In two hours and a bit, three at the outside, the icon had been cleaned, but was not gleaming. Or if it was, it was a very dull gleam. Seryozha was already weaving spells with his brushes, applying paint, and relegating the now redundant Skunk completely to the background. He deftly coloured the white patches, toning them in with the overall background, and then set to work describing the haloes using a compass with a special little beak-like paintpot on the end.

"There, see. You give them a halo and the face cheers up immediately. Who's this we've got here? Ruch, the righteous robber who was going to be first into Paradise, eh? Right, let's renovate him. You see what the halo does? It draws your attention, concentrates it, and the panel, you see, provides a framework, the strip round the edge of the panel holds the space together, organizes it in other words."

Skunk did not really understand all this learned chatter, but he could see how the restored, bright circles really did bring the icon amazingly to life, and the angels' wings acquired a new lightness and an elegant curve which the grime and wear of the years had obscured. The point of the compass was jabbed unceremoniously into the forehead or the bridge of the nose of a face, even if it was the countenance of Christ Himself. A flourish, and an evenly gleaming circle of light, bluish, white, sometimes pink, appeared above the head, and it began to look good, seeming to stand out from the panel and drawing the eye to it.

As Seryozha worked he talked, obviously for the benefit of Aunt Vera, who had crept up into the light and was now standing behind his back:

"This, then, is the Second Coming, also called The Last Judgement, painted from the prophecy of Daniel and the Book of Revelations."

Seryozha was on home ground here. He knew the subject backwards and could make everything fall into place.

In the centre at the top Christ the Saviour, the Dread Judge, was seated on the throne. To left and right, falling at his feet, Adam and Eve with her flowing tresses gestured towards him. To either side there stood, or more exactly, flowed towards the centre, as if on an iconostasis, the Mother of God, John the Baptist emaciated from his stay in the wilderness, Saints Peter and Paul, and all the other figures after them.

"The deisis is a prayer for the future," the requisite commentary was obligingly provided. Beneath the throne mighty

Moses was clutching a scroll with the Ten Commandments in one hand, and using the other to pull the beard of a desperately yelling Pharisee with bulging fish eyes who had got himself entangled in the folds of his own robe. They were being viewed dispassionately by several crowds, the peoples of the Earth congregating in readiness for Judgement. On the left side they were counterbalanced by other crowds, the demure, motionless ranks of the saints, archpriests, priests, and martyrs for the faith. From both sides the ranks directed their attentive eyes to the throne like a field of closely planted sunflowers.

From the foot of the throne there flowed a fiery river alongside which, repeating the line of its course, a fat-bellied, hideous coiled serpent was being cast down. Each of its coils was emblazoned with a special sin: pride, envy, gluttony, covetousness, foul language, fornication, violence, perfidy, slander, drunkenness, blasphemy, avarice, vanity, self-love, and the sin against the Holy Ghost, which was the final coil before the bloated body reached the fiery head, its jaws spread wide in the unbearable heat of the fires of Gehenna. There, in Hell, amid the flames of the raging fires, red and large, with his ribs sticking out, sat Satan with a little person on his knees. This was the black soul of the traitor Judas. Here too, in these realms of fire, in four circles, furiously rolling their eyes, their jaws wide open, their paws raised menacingly, were four fearsome beasts: the four kingdoms of the Antichrist. A little further away and separately, also framed in medallions, the Earth and the Seas gave up their dead, disgorging them in their thousands, the bodies contorted and crushed and flying down into a hideous nightmarish abyss, to Judgement. Right at the bottom, in the very bowels of Hell, in black and brown flowers with sharp thorns, naked, chortling, vile demons and imps were tormenting howling and groaning sinners, whose eyes were popping out of their heads in anguish, their tongues bitten and swollen. They were being scourged, torn, bitten, and sawn with sharp saws by special sawing demons with hairy bellies, their live, suffering flesh branded with glowing irons. To the left, above the vile, blazing Hell, stinking of brimstone and excrement, an Angel with a lance was dispatching the serpentine figure of Death, which was writhing like a worm on coals of fire. And immediately above them and slightly to one side, the pandemonium disappeared entirely, giving way to the pastel and serenely flowing lines of Paradise where Daniel, leaning like an infant against the Archangel Gabriel, was gazing at the horrors beneath and heeding his explanations. The Archangel's finger was pointing at each and all of them together: the heretics burning for all eternity, the turbanned Indians, the negroes with their outturned lips, the moon-faced, crafty saracens in brocade coats, the archbishops with their *klobuks* on their heads who had transgressed against their vows, the pagan renegates Arius, Nestorius and Macedonius, goatee bearded, their hair in disarray and already smouldering at the sides of their faces.

The tribe of Abraham had been painted in next to Daniel, tranquil, welcoming, cascading like grapes on a pillar, with the hosts of the righteous reclining there, all those who had entered Paradise before the creation of the Kingdom of Heaven: silver-haired Siv, Moses and the first soul, Ruch the robber, with the kindly face of a confectioner and baker. Above them, even higher, up towards the top of the panel, in a fragrant mansion, sat the Mother of God, the Madonna, on cushions sewn with river pearls, beneath sky-blue vaults as ethereal as a silken canopy.

Along the sides of the icon, in elongated, chiselled seals, there rode on clouds monks who had attained sanctity and, first among them, bushy browed and bearded Balaam, and the Indian prince he had christened and received into the monkhood, Josaph, wearing his turban with a huge precious stone, having given away his parent's treasure to the poor and withdrawn with his teacher's blessing into a vocation of healing and reclusiveness. There floated also Zosima and

Savvaty of Solovki, and Saint Sergius of Radonezh the miracle-worker, and the young, locally venerated Ioann and Yakov of Menyuzh who had perished through misunderstanding, and the boy Artemy Verkolsky, miraculously killed by a thunderbolt in the fields. They were transported to a place of ineffable beauty, to the Heavenly City of Jerusalem in whose palaces and mansions there dwelt the heavenly sages. And with them, as if climbing a ladder, surrounded by a cloud of radiance, Christ was rising to His Father to take His place at His right hand.

Immediately alongside, but slightly lower, the Archangel Michael in the ascetic schema of a monk was defeating the legions of Satan, casting them down into Hell, surrounded all about by the chanting legions of heaven.

Thus, along an unhurried, smooth line which occasionally plunged headlong, the denizens of Paradise travelled, as did the loathesome, naked, shameful demons, all in a great wheel, like the inexorable passage of time, and there, up in the uppermost lefthand corner was a little door where the Heavenly Jerusalem was revealed, but even above and beyond that, there was a place for new heavens, radiant with light, impossible either for the eye to see or the mind to grasp.

Seryozha varnished the panel, systematically covering it with a broad brush, and everything that Skunk had seen suddenly glowed more strongly, loading the eye even more powerfully, attracting and repelling independently of the will. Aunt Vera, transfixed with horror, her face ashen, could not take her eyes off the icon, and Skunk too had evidently taken it to heart, because the restorer suddenly lost patience and hissed at them, "What are you goggling at, you sad people? Are you scared?" Aunt Vera, as always, took the question personally, and responded as always with a tear and a sigh, which at least helped her out of her stupor. Skunk reacted differently, however. He suddenly took offence and went off into the depths of the refectory, sat down in a chair, and

stared fixedly at the empty eye sockets of Adam's shinily
varnished wooden skull beneath the base of the Cross and, as
always, stuck his thumb in his mouth.

10

Then something extraordinary happened to him, like a dream,
except that it was no dream.

At the start he could still clearly see the restorer whose
offhand jibe had so offended him bent over by the lamp, but
then the light began to dim, to dissolve, and a veil seemed to
come down in front of his eyes. And there really was a veil,
even a kind of glass dome, hard to the touch and squeaking
like window glass under a fingernail. He found himself immured
in glass and at first struggled, beating against the walls of his
prison with his hands and feet and even his head; but they
were unyielding, and having worn himself out, he retreated,
weary and frightened, sat down on the stone floor (the chair
had also disappeared), and found himself suddenly plunged
in total darkness.

Yet at the same time the sun was clearly shining. He could
feel its rays on his body, his bare neck, his face, together with
a suffocating, unendurable, hellish heat. He could not see. He
could not see anything around him. He had gone blind. It was
odd that he was not afraid, simply accepting everything as it
was, putting his trust in a sudden certainty that all was as it
should be. To compensate for his lost sight, his ears and
nostrils came suddenly alive as they breathed in strange air,
and told him that the sea or an ocean was near at hand, so
strong, so unmistakable was the salty, iodine tang of seaweed.

The sea was not far away. He could hear the sound of
the breakers and went towards it following a clifftop path. The
clay beneath his feet was firm, only here and there made
slippery by draining rainwater, and he walked along, stepping
confidently but without haste, in order not to catch his toe in a

pothole and hurtle down the sheer drop. His weight was being shifted on to his toes, the stones bit into them painfully, but he went on down, closer and closer until, rounding a last turn in the path, he felt the full force of the salty wind blowing strongly, stubbornly in his face, and knew he was on the beach.

A storm was brewing out at sea, nothing too fierce, but the waves were dashing noisily against the sand and hissing as they drew back again. He decided to stay on the beach for a while, and walked on to the sand. His feet immediately sank into it. He took off his trainers to feel it hot on his bare feet, and grains of sand immediately stuck to his sweaty skin. There was a sudden scuffling and something rained down on him from above. Somebody was standing up there, and as soon as he sprang away from the cliff face, there came a low, blood-curdling growl from up there. The wind diminished the effect, but it was clear enough that up there in the place he had just descended from, something loathsome was watching and stalking him, and perhaps even hunting him, helpless in his blindness.

"Who is it up there?" he asked the emptiness in front of him, not expecting a reply; but the reply came directly inside his head. A kind, gentle voice replied, a little languidly, "The demons with sharp saws."

Already Skunk could differentiate their voices. Not one, but a whole pack of them were singing the song of the chase, which ended in repulsive, rasping giggles. He suddenly saw them distinctly in his mind's eye, half-human, half-dog, standing on all fours on the clifftop, covered in hair in front, bare and slippery smooth behind, with long, thin rats' tails. The wind carried the stench from their jaws down to him. Skunk could even hear their heavy breathing, and shuddered at the sound of their great fangs snapping.

"What should I do? What will there be after this?" he asked his unseen guide uncertainly.

"Go fearlessly, go to your end, and you will rest and rise

again to receive your just reward at the end of days," the strange voice echoed in his head.

There was no going back, so he must go forward into the sea. He lost all control of himself. He was drawn to the water, he so wanted to experience the unprecedented sensation of battling with the elements. His common sense abandoned him. He was no longer thinking about the strange words, or indeed about anything else. He stepped fearlessly forward, and the sea flowed round him,cascades of brine: an incoming wave almost knocked him off his feet, soaked him up to the knees, and dragged him after it. He leapt back and threw off his clothes. The howling and mayhem behind his back grew louder, as if the beasts were lamenting a prey which was escaping them.

He threw himself into the waves, feeling the slap of the water with his whole body. He was immediately sucked down to the bottom, gravel flaying his skin, and it seemed that a stupid and inglorious end was nigh: but at the last moment he caught hold of a great rock firmly anchored in the sea. Skunk held on tightly, wrapping his arms and legs round this fortuitous stone,and keeping his eyes and lips firmly closed. He could neither stand nor sit. One wave hurled itself at him after another, turning him, cutting off his air for a moment, tugging, sucking him down into the deep,scouring a mass of sand and grit back and forth over his body, as if determined that if it could not detach him, it would at least polish him to a high shine. It seemed that at any moment an exceptional wave might come and tear him off and he would be ground to pieces and he strained every nerve, but the elements again drew back. He began to feel terror, but at the same time wild exhilaration. He seemed to be hurtling somewhere on the wet rock, without knowing why or where to. He swallowed a considerable quantity of salt water and felt freezing cold: he knew he ought to struggle back to the shore, but he constantly had the feeling that only here, on this rock, was he safe, and that otherwise he was sure to be washed away and dragged to the bottom of the sea. His body was aching terribly, his muscles had gone numb, but still he lay (or was he sailing?) on his ship, and this went on for a long time before he finally gathered enough courage to relinquish his grip and dash back on buckling legs to the shore as an especially ferocious wave was flooding back.

He collapsed exhausted on the hot sand, unable to gather himself together, unable to get warm, but nevertheless comforted somewhat by the boldness of his achievement. He had survived, once again he had survived. The satanic baying was no longer to be heard overhead, and the unseen guide who had prompted him to take the plunge so strangely had disappeared also, and gave no response despite his entreaties.

Suddenly everything else disappeared too: the blazing sun; the beach with its hot sand; and all that remained was the chill in his heart and the salty, iodine taste on his dry lips. Slowly, painfully, he regained his sight and was again sitting in the chair in his corner of the church, and the darkness was now only in the eye sockets of the polished skull of Adam; but it was an irredeemable darkness, and with it fear and despair crept into his soul. A sense of desolation and futility overwhelmed him.

11

With the corner of his eye or, more likely, with his keen ear, he detected the reawakening of the church. The iron grating at the main door rasped and was pushed back. Like pale shadows one, two, three of the daytime old women materialized, and without delay started moving things about, carrying, polishing. One of them came over to his corner and lit a first candle, left there yesterday for just that purpose. The grey-black muffled figure shot a glance at him with a beady, mouse-like eye and, starting back in fright, scurried away into the depths of the church.

The women changed the holiday icon on the lectern by the high altar, and mopped and scrubbed their way from the interior towards the doors. He could clearly see Seryozha bending at the trestle, putting the final touches to his magic beside the lamp, whose light paled in the sunlight streaming through a small window. But the main door was thrown open and in the entrance arch appeared the figure of the priest, flabby cheeked, pot-bellied, kindly, radiating goodwill, and with a long, greasy pigtail flowing down over the collar of his wing sleeved vestment. The old women, abandoning their brushes and mops, ran over to kiss his hand, squawking like sparrows being fed, and the devout priest greeted each of them individually, bowed, made the sign of the Cross over them and, quaintly offering them his great fist, marched over to the restorer.

"Have you finished your work, my son?" his voice boomed out to every corner of the church. It was a magnificent voice, morning fresh and full of joy.

"It's all yours, Father Trifon."

Skunk listened as the usual haggling began, the restorer jokily praising his own work, Father Trifon looking for oversights but failing to find any, and therefore loudly smacking his lips, rubbing his hands, cracking his fingers as a preliminary to explaining the icon to the women crowding round, dwelling particularly on the torments of hell. They nodded meekly, whispering among themselves and making the sign of the Cross. Another priest came in unnoticed, the one with the short hair who had officiated at the cemetery. Seryozha, who was quite giggly in the presence of the amiable Trifon, for some reason now put on an expression of meekness, bowed, and sidled over to kiss the hand of the new arrival. The commissioning of the icon continued, but not for long. The priest from the cemetery, Father Boris his parishioners called him, took a quick glance and gestured dismissively, as if to say, "Fine!" before going off towards the altar or into it. Father Trifon, on the other hand, now began his round of the church, crossing himself pensively and at length before each icon. Skunk followed him with his eyes unwaveringly, tensely, waiting for this kind-faced priest to come level with the Crucifix. Everything in his appearance, loving, intense without being severe, instilled trust, and made Skunk like him.

Then something incredible happened. Some force suddenly impelled Skunk out of his chair and threw him to the ground, down on his knees. He crawled to the priest, beating his head on the ground, hard, loudly, but without feeling any pain. He was trembling all over, sweat broke out on his forehead, he couldn't keep his teeth from chattering, and finally, as if a dam had burst, the words came flooding out with a moan: "Father, Father, forgive me, forgive me. I have sinned. I have sinned." While he was crawling from his wall Father Trifon, who had at first recoiled in alarm, recovered his composure, smiled, opened his arms and stood waiting for him. But Skunk, unseeing, impervious, stubbornly focussed on the hem of his cassock and, burying his face in it, clutched the bottom of the priest's vestment and, convulsively pulling it towards him, only whispered in a flat, hoarse voice, "Forgive me, forgive me, I have sinned, Father. I have killed a man, I have sent another to his death. I have stolen. I am a thief. Father, forgive me."

Again and again he repeated, or rather, muttered the same thing, losing his drift, muddled, over and over again endlessly, like a formula he had learned long ago, but now there was no making out the words. His strength had gone from him and he was lying on the floor, on the pleasantly cooling stone slabs, and only his hands, like an anchor, having caught the material, would not let go and tugged at the cassock, causing the priest a good deal of embarrassment: and his heart pounded in a frenzy in his breast.

"Control yourself, young man, control yourself," the priest urged him anxiously, but seeing that words were of no avail, called for help. The old ladies bestirred themselves and brought a glass of water, but now Skunk's legs began to twitch and, at the end of his strength, he kept repeating the same words, "I have sinned, I have sinned, forgive me, Father."

The other priest, Boris, came running, caught Skunk under the arms, and managed to pull him off the distraught Trifon, helped him to the door and out into the fresh air.

"Come on, come on, old chap, use your legs, you'll feel better when you've had a breath of fresh air," he said to the half-demented Skunk, but whether comforting or merely humouring him was not clear.

Skunk collapsed into his waiting embrace, but moved his legs going down the steps, made it to the churchyard and allowed himself to be sat down on a bench. Here he was about to succumb to another fit, but by a miracle he caught what Father Trifon was saying to the lady churchwarden. "Go quickly, we need either psychiatric help or the police. Go and phone them, for God's sake." His inner alarm bell started ringing. He was already recovering his breath, he had relaxed, taken the ladle of water in his hands and drunk it, spilling only a little.

Now, without listening to what the priests and solicitous old ladies were wittering at him from both sides, well aware that they were just trying to humour him until the men in white coats arrived or, worse, the police, cursing their meanness of spirit in his heart, he focussed all his remaining strength and suddenly, with a loud yell, taking them completely by surprise, waving his arms, jumped up, broke through their cordon and rushed from the churchyard, tumbled headlong down the steps to the river and, keeping to the undergrowth, making a wide detour, headed back to his hideaway at the pumping station collapsing, in total exhaustion, on to the dirty bed and falling into a deep, empty sleep close to total blackout.

He must have slept an hour or an hour and a half, but it was enough to bring him back to his senses. A terrible weariness, resulting from his night-time vigil by the icon, or more exactly from a sickness which had suddenly come on him and deprived him of his usual circumspection, a clouding of his heart and mind (he was acutely aware that his heart had had quite a say in the whole business, so strangely had it fluttered in his chest beside the candlestand), had all now drained and passed away, thank God; he again felt strength in his limbs, and he was thinking clearly. His sense of danger had saved the day again. A fine figure he would be cutting now on a bunk at the police station, and although he was fairly sure they would not have managed to beat a confession out of him, they might well have framed him for someone else's misdeed, something they were famous for.

Skunk looked in amazement at his reflection in the fragment of mirror on the wall. His face seemed little different from how it had looked yesterday or the day before, but why on earth had he been so stupid and irrational as to trust the priests? "Go quickly. We need either psychiatric help or the police. Go and phone them, for God's sake!" "You goats!" He gave a twisted smile, but suddenly again vividly recalled the icon, the restorer humming cheerfully to himself, and the emotion, inexplicably deep, like the fear of sudden death, which seemed not entirely to have left him even now.

As always when life had driven him into a corner, he began to sort through his possibilities at lightning speed. It was too dangerous to go home at present. Aunt Vera might have mentioned his name and, although the probability was low, he had no intention of taking the risk. In any case, the familiar, all-devouring anger was beginning to simmer so delightfully inside him that he seemed at last to be coming up with something.

He patted the pockets of his jacket and pulled out the crushed banknotes. It was all there. He retrieved the briefcase from its hiding place, tidily packed wad after wad into it, pulled out of a plank in the wall a long thin awl with a wooden handle, ran his nail over its tip and found it satisfactorily sharp, and threw it too into the case. Then he went outside. He sneaked back to the church through allotments and byways he had known since childhood and settled down in the currant and raspberry bushes, his eyes fixed on the door. If he was in luck and the one with short hair, Father Boris, was still there, he would follow him home and pay him a surprise visit. Father Trifon... well, Father Trifon could wait. He would think up something special for him. It was this one, though, the one who ripped off penniless old women, that he wanted to sort things out with just as soon as he could.

As always when he was hiding, waiting to follow someone, he was heedless of the passing of time or discomfort. Only those big ears of his which had more than once been the saving of him, were sensitively attuned to any possible danger, but everything was fine. The service was over, everyone had come out of the church and gone home, and then, finally, Father Boris appeared surrounded by old women and that scrawny, pockmarked sexton who evidently looked after him. Skunk realized now that Father Boris must be a monk.

Having bade his old ladies farewell, the monk strode out of the churchyard and turned into a side street. Scurrying behind him and a little to one side came the sexton. They did not talk as they walked: Father Boris was evidently lost in contemplation. Skunk crept out of the bushes and stealthily, invisibly, followed them to a perfectly ordinary wooden house which stood in a row of other such private houses. Then he stole into the small, neglected garden overgrown with weeds and hid behind a long disused and leaning shed. It was clear that Father Boris was no gardener. The sexton came out to the yard several times, carrying a bucket full of rubbish, heaving water indoors from the pump, and soon, it was already towards evening, came on to the porch, straightened her headscarf, and called back into the hallway, "Well I'll be off now, Father. See you tomorrow!" and, without waiting for a reply, came down from the wooden verandah and banged the gate.

Skunk peeped out from behind the shed. He held the briefcase out in front of himself. It was to be the first thing Father Boris would see. The owl, he checked, was lying on top of the money. He would be able to get hold of it instantly. He went up on to the porch and knocked three times at the door.

"Come in, it isn't locked," the priest responded.

Skunk threw open the door and went in.

13

Oddly enough, Skunk was expecting something else. Father Boris at home wasn't wearing his priestly vestments: he was in a light dressing gown which barely covered his knees and was open at the chest where, in a thick growth of greying hairs, there dangled on a cord, no cross, but a pendant apparently made of lead. It looked a bit like a torpedo. He seemed very much at home with worn slippers on his bare feet. Father Boris stood in the doorway of his room peering at his visitor, his eyes screwed up as he looked into the light from the dark corridor. For a moment he seemed at a loss. He had probably been expecting someone else and, seeing Skunk and not being particularly aware of who it was, he suddenly blushed childishly and darted quickly into a small room to one side, saying as he disappeared, "Forgive me. I'm not properly dressed. Because of the heat. Do go through. I'll be with you in a minute."

His flight, his failure to recognize the seriousness of the moment (Skunk had after all been relying on the effect the briefcase would have, but Father Boris seemed not even to have noticed it), his somehow very human, even infantile behaviour, drained Skunk of his truculence and, having quite lost momentum, he shifted from foot to foot in the hallway. The damned briefcase, to say nothing of the owl, was immediately so beside the point that he did not know what to do with it; but it would have been even more ridiculous just to leave. He had no option but to go into the round sitting room with its big table piled with books, papers, envelopes with bright, manifestly foreign stamps, with a glass dish full of buttery biscuits, and a bar of chocolate with a bite out of it. While he was looking round Father Boris apologized once more from behind the curtain. He was in no hurry in there, but was also making no attempt to keep track of what Skunk was doing. The curtain covered the opening securely. In order to get a grip on himself Skunk started looking round the walls. They were lined with books, but these were plainly in some disorder. Moreover, the shelves had not been bought but built to order as new books arrived, which created an untidy but impressive effect. There were fat books and thin books, books in shiny foreign jackets, and books which had foreign lettering directly on the spine. They were mostly new, although a multi-volume Bible had found a place, as had some others with Church Slavonic script which he was unable to read. On a table under the mirror stood a porcelain Virgin Mary, unfamiliarly white with painted loving eyes, a little nose, a little mouth; and a similarly porcelain Jesus with, for some reason, his body opened up to reveal his heart licked by tongues of flame in the chest cavity. Jesus was looking at him with his head inclined slightly downwards and holding back his clothing with his hands. There were several other pictures, cut out of magazines, stuck on the walls with drawing pins. They were odd. Plainly religious, but somehow not like icons, even though the people in them had golden haloes, and several of them evidently depicted Christ and the Virgin.

"How about some tea?" he suddenly heard from behind his back.

124

Skunk jumped up without letting go of the briefcase, and stared at Father Boris who by now was wearing his cassock, albeit without the big pectoral cross on the chain. He was holding a five pint aluminium kettle no less awkwardly than Skunk was holding the ill-starred briefcase. For some moments they looked only at each other's hands, and Skunk suddenly seized up. All he had planned, all the words he had prepared, accumulated and lined up in his brain, suddenly evaporated and his whole body started shaking again, right to the tips of his fingers. As a result he said, no doubt in desperation, something quite inane:

"Oh, please. That would be nice."

"Splendid. I won't be a moment." Father Boris disappeared into the kitchen, rattled around at the stove, came back into the room and, indicating a chair, relieved Skunk of the briefcase.

"So, you decided to give it back? Well, good luck to it."

He put it to one side on the sofa, settled himself comfortably next to it, in the corner by the bolster, looked up and gazed searchingly at his visitor.

"So, you believe in Christ?" he asked unexpectedly, like a schoolmaster.

Skunk looked down. He should have jumped up, run out. His ears were ablaze as merrily as the heart of the painted figurine. But he could not.

"So, you do believe," the monk nailed him. "That's the main thing. Incidentally, I should really take the money to the church treasurer, but perhaps I don't need to," he added, by now with a smile. "I imagine, though, there was something you wanted to ask about."

Skunk clammed up even tighter.

"Never mind." Seeing his hesitancy Father Boris adopted a kindlier, less didactic tone. "I expect you were indignant with Father Trifon today. Don't try to deny it, I can read it in your eyes. You shouldn't be. You must forgive him. The poor

125

man was merely acting from habit, and also he lost his head. To tell the truth, you gave us a fright this morning. Are you by any chance ill?"

Skunk could barely restrain his trembling, but remained obstinately silent. Then Father Boris got up, walked about the room, took a small picture book from the table and held it out to Skunk.

"Take a look while we're waiting for the kettle to boil and I am out in the kitchen. If you want anything, call me."

As if nothing happened, he went out leaving Skunk on his own. The trembling gradually subsided. Skunk recognized that he was not going to be shouted at here, and his curiosity took the upper hand. He looked at the book, but decided against opening it. It was a children's Bible with a lamb, Christ and the Virgin Mary on its glossy red cover.

He carried on sitting there, not moving a hair, waiting, for some reason inwardly certain that sitting and waiting was the right thing to do. Father Boris seemed to have taken away his willpower with his unusual behaviour. At last the priest brought through the hot kettle, took cups out of a cupboard, and poured tea for himself and Skunk.

"Right, get stuck in, and you really must try the biscuits. My mum sent them from Petersburg. Help yourself. Do you like chocolate?" He broke off the bit with the toothmarks, popped it in his mouth, and munched with relish.

Skunk managed to blurt out, "No, thanks," moved his tea cup nearer and started stirring it.

"Have some sugar, have some sugar, my little robber," Father Boris shouted at him, by now wholly at ease, and this made Skunk feel really terrible; but still he did not walk out, only sat dipping his lip in the sweet tea out of politeness, and making no move towards the biscuits or chocolate. Father Boris, as if forgetting him, opened a small book, arranged himself comfortably opposite him, and settled down to read, from time to time sipping a little tea, breaking a few squares of the chocolate and putting them in his mouth. The silence became unbearable. It was obvious he ought to leave, but Skunk seemed riveted to the chair, and who knows how it would all have ended if there had not suddenly come a knock at the door.

"Come in, it's open," Father Boris responded, and got up to greet his visitor, gesturing to Skunk to remain seated.

It was Seryozha, the restorer. He nodded to Skunk from the doorway as if he was an old friend, and handed the priest a large fish wrapped in stout brown paper.

"It's a chub, Father. May it keep you in good health."

"Good, good, thank you for that. I am very partial to fish," the monk said, clearly pleased. "Put it through in the kitchen, will you? The woman will come tomorrow and cook it. It's a sin how much I like fried fish. Only, will it keep till tomorrow?"

"Of course. It needs to be gutted and put in the fridge..."

"Oh, dear. That's something," Father Boris said in embarrassment, "that I am really not very good at."

"I'll fry it for you," Skunk volunteered, surprising himself.

"Splendid. Can you sort everything out for yourself in the kitchen?" The monk made no attempt to conceal his relief. They changed places: Skunk went out to the kitchen, and Seryozha and the priest went back to the sitting room.

Skunk took the big chub, which weighed around five and a half pounds, outside in order not to make a mess on the table, and cut it up on a board in the kitchen garden. Only when he had the pieces of fish in the frying pan and had put on a fresh kettle of water did he move a little way out of the door into the corridor and covertly, unnoticed, eavesdropped on their conversation.

Father Boris was on the attack, furiously hurling his words as if out to nail his opponent.

"No, no, Seryozha, that is not true. I understood back in the seminary that only ecumenism will do. Peter is the rock, on him Christ established his Church, and that means that Rome is the true centre of Christianity. That's right, that's absolutely right. When I was still a novice with Nikanor I realized things had to be more rigorous. I had to have status. I wanted to become a bishop, which is why I graduated from the Academy. I longed ardently to reunite the churches from above into one body of Christ. Now I have come down in the world. When Nikanor died they packed me off to Pazaran, to the outlying regions of Stargorod. Did I complain? There are people there who worship the sun and trees to this day. And is it any better here? Take that rock. What a joke. He sailed here on a rock! An Italian professor came here last year, examined the stone, and was in ecstasies. It's all a lot of complete twaddle. Believe it or not, this rock is a Sicilian variety. In the middle ages it was used as ballast in the holds of ships. So there was a ship, it rotted away, and their magic rock is still here. But will they believe it? You should hear them, Seryozha."

"I've been listening to them since I was a child, Father. After all, I'm a local lad. What if it was ballast: the main thing is that he sailed here. And whether it was on a ship or a rock is just a detail of faith, nothing more."

"But ideas don't just come from nowhere! Orthodox priests have dreamt all this up. He came, he heard, he believed, as if Orthodoxy gets poured in through your ears. But Catholicism is rational, you understand it with your mind. No, look, you have come to Christ, you have thought it through, first and foremost you have thought it out with your brains, comparing what made sense and what did not. And only then were you christened, am I right?"

"Well, not really, Father Boris. It was much less elegant than that: I believed and so on, and only started reading books afterwards."

"I don't deny Christ calls all manner of men, but we are not talking about you and me. All around us is a swamp, and the frightening thing is that it swallows people up. No, at least

128

Pazaran had tranquillity: Stargorod is relatively bustling. You feel closer to St Petersburg here, nearer to Moscow too. The air is different. No, my dear Seryozha, this is not ambition, but truth! And at least the Catholics tell you openly that if you want to break away you're out on your ear. They have the Vatican, which, incidentally, is a state. While in Russia we are constantly under the heel of the secular state, constantly under threat from informers."

"Father Boris, Father Boris, wait. You take everything too far. Suppose it is just a swamp all around us, but, forgive me, for God's sake, you are a monk, you have a bishop over you, and a duty of obedience..."

"Stop, stop. Obedience? Who says I don't accept my duty of obedience? My bishop is a Catholic bishop in Lithuania. I travel to him for confession. You know, when Nikanor died I held my tongue, I kept my head down at first, but I am not afraid now. Times are changing. Freedom is too frightening. I am not even afraid of excommunication. I probably will leave here quite soon. I shall go to Rome to study, and after that I shall return to start everything from scratch again, only this time no longer in secret, but shouting at the top of my voice; one drop at a time, you know, constant dripping wears away the stone. There!" He threw the word out, and immediately launched into a new attack. "There are intelligent people even here who understand intellectually that the Church should be united and strong. Otherwise, and this is terrible but true, we are talking about surrender: surrender to the enemy of mankind. You hadn't thought of that? Listen, I was really stumped by this one for a long time, but there is evidence. You don't by any chance read German? No? Too bad. An extremely clever man, despite the fact that he is a Protestant, opened my eyes with his explanation of where all the horrors of this century have come from. You won't deny, I'm sure, that our century has been something out of the ordinary. But it's all perfectly straightforward. Satan has rented the Earth from God on a

129

hundred year lease! At first I thought it was complete nonsense, but the more I thought about it the more I became convinced that, cruel and terrible as it might seem, it was the truth. Stalin, Hitler, Auschwitz, the labour camps of Kolyma, the atom bomb; and you'll notice that as soon as things eased off a little in the outside world, we discovered a threat coming from within: AIDS for our sins. That's more effective than any bomb. And whose hands is that the work of? The Unclean Spirit, of course, no one else. It has all come to pass. You just have to know how to read properly. The fourth Kingdom as described in the Book of Daniel. But our century is coming to a close, Seryozha, and we shall be the judges who will take power away from the beast. We, not they, not today's clergy, will make the Church strong. Am I not right?"

"Oh, Father, words can be found by all and sundry to support any view; people differ, but the Church is one. And people, including, incidentally, today's clergy, have preserved her."

"Folly. Everything is through God's providence. They have ruined everything."

"Forgive me, Father, but the people never lost faith. Fair enough, until the thunder comes the peasant will not cross himself, but then he will cross himself, not do namaz like some Mohammedan. It's a matter of natural, traditional faith."

"Stop, stop, stop! Faith in magic rocks, or faith in Christ Jesus?"

"Their magic rock is a tradition. It is only a crutch for their faith, something that belongs to the age, to the age of their parents, their grandfathers and great grandmothers. What's wrong with that?"

"What age? What history? Russians do not know their own history; they positively despise it. No, in Soviet terms we were big, but in reality, in reality we were just a gap, a negative, something that never happened. To tell the truth, I feel tired. I am forty years old, I have started going grey, and what have

I to show for it? Should I wait around like Trifon for better times to come? Faith without works is dead! I, I will create a real Russian Catholic Church, strong as granite, rigorous; all we have here at present is just debility and tears."

"Father, Father, stop. Think what you are saying! There may be things I do not understand, but I feel..." In Seryozha's words Skunk detected an authentic note of horror. "For heaven's sake, this is the sin of pride speaking in you. It is an illness. You are a monk, I am a lay person, but the things you are saying to me... No, I am a bad Christian, I admit it, but I am quite certain that no Catholic in his right mind would accept you. You have simply dreamed all this up. We are dealing with life on this earth, but you have nothing but abstract ideas. People are waiting for you. People here love you. I talked to the women..."

"They would love a hollow tree if you put a cassock on it."

"Then that is what they need. Are you there to serve them, or are they there to serve you?"

"Precisely so, my dear Seryozha. You simply have not yet understood fully. I am on their side, it is all for their sake. After all, I am a pure Russian, so I must suffer for them. Jesus is calling me."

At just that moment there was a smell of something burning. Skunk rushed back to the stove and turned off the gas, but didn't dare go and interrupt their arguing. He had understood almost nothing, but recognized that, like good Russians, they were talking extremes, which meant it was coming straight from the heart. Fortunately, Father Boris had heard the commotion in the kitchen and appeared, almost too quickly, in the door, as if he no longer wished to be on his own with the restorer.

"Everything ready?"

"It's got a bit burned."

"Never mind, I can tell from the smell it's divine. Bring it through! Seryozha, will you have some of the fish with us?"

Seryozha did not reply. He was sitting looking downcast on the edge of his chair and nodded, probably out of politeness, but did not speak. Father Boris, on the other hand, piled up whole mountains of steaming fish fillets for himself and Skunk and started eating quickly and deftly, saying how good it was and smacking his lips.

"There, you see, I'm no good at cooking it, but a virtuoso when it comes to eating it!"

He really was getting through the big head like a full-time fisherman. He sucked out the eyes, bit out the cheeks, then slurped the brain marrow before sucking every bone so infectiously that Skunk, who was starving, fell upon his own helping and demolished it at lightning speed.

"Why so crestfallen, Seryozha? Think, think. Young people like you and me are supposed to think and act and try to enlighten dunderheads like... I hope you aren't offended?!" he said winking at Skunk. "Where do you live?"

"Oh, just..."

"Look, you can sleep here on my sofa. There's plenty of room." Father Boris seemed able to read his thoughts: "Problems at home, I dare say?"

"Uhuh," Skunk was happy to admit it. Father Boris, chewing the fish head with such enjoyment, Father Boris who had forgiven him for the briefcase, who had forgiven him everything, who had not said a single word of reproach, had won his heart. As to what they had been arguing about, Catholics, rocks, he had only gathered that Seryozha had somehow been at fault, and Father Boris had been at fault over something else, and he liked the fact that now they were both repenting. It warmed his heart very much more than the usual drunk's "I like you. You respect me..."; or his mother's loving tears which were invariably a prelude to a fit of hysterics and not infrequently getting his ears boxed into the bargain. And then, of course, just the fact that suddenly here was a monk talking (to him!) and inviting him to stay the night.

132

"That's agreed! Now let's have some tea with raspberries, eh?" Father Boris started pouring, but Seryozha got up and bowed.

"Forgive me, Father, I think I'll be off. I have to get to the far side of town. Perhaps I could just have a quick sip of water."

He quickly drank the ladle dry, and then stood shifting from one foot to the other at the door.

"Well, God speed!" Father Boris put his arms round Seryozha and they kissed in parting. "We've just been finding our range so far. We've still a lot to talk about. I haven't upset you?"

"No, of course not, Father Boris. Believe me, I really mean it. It's just that I don't believe, it's even rather frightening somehow, you ought to..."

"Of course, of course. I didn't just think it all up today, you know," the monk patted his shoulder pedagogically. "God speed, come again tomorrow, or any other time for that matter, okay? The house is open to you, since we are not enemies, and that is wonderful. But I'll break you yet. We Catholics only come once, but we stay for eternity."

He threw open the door, stood a little while for appearances' sake, and then turned round to Skunk.

"Let's finish our tea quickly, gather everything up and clear it away to the kitchen. The woman will wash up tomorrow. Then we'll make up the beds and sleep!"

He got out clean sheets and, seeing that Skunk was hesitant, gave him a rather strange look.

"What is it? Are you afraid of me?"

"'Course not."

"Quite right. Into bed then."

Under his quizzical gaze Skunk undressed down to his shorts and dived under the blanket.

"Sleep well, God be with you. The toilet is in the corridor on the right." Father Boris made the sign of the Cross on

Skunk's forehead, retreated into his little room, and pulled the curtain to behind him.

14

What he was doing behind the curtain, whether he was praying or just lying on his bed, Skunk could not hear. At first there was dead silence in the house, but not for long. Father Boris could not sleep, and neither could he. The priest was pacing about in there, his dressing gown rustling. Skunk knew that he was pacing from one corner to the other and, finally, the curtain rings rattled back along the metal rail. Father Boris looked in on him.

"Are you asleep?"

"No, I can't."

"Well there we are, neither can I. You probably heard what Seryozha and I were talking about, but did you understand?"

"No, not really."

"Never mind. I can't sleep, Daniil, because I have great plans."

He shifted his shoulders and inclined his head slightly, instantly reverting to his schoolmaster mode. He was suddenly just a bit over-earnest, a bit too tiresomely strict; and when he began to talk, the tone was again as didactic as at the beginning, when he had asked Skunk whether he believed in Christ.

"Have you ever heard of the Pope? Of course you have, but to you that all seems very far away. I don't suppose you have even read the Gospels, have you?"

"No. Where would I... "

"That is bad, very bad, but we shall put everything to rights, have no fear. Well then, there is a person on Earth called the Pope. He's the head of the whole of the Catholic Church. The Catholic Church is very strong: there are Catholics

134

in every country. Long, long ago all Christians were together in a single church, but very stupidly, because of people's pride, many centuries ago the churches divided. One, the western one, is the Catholic Church; the other, the eastern one, is Orthodoxy. And in all this time they haven't managed to get together again."

"But why should they?" Skunk ventured, raising himself on the pillows and sitting up in bed.

"Precisely! Many people think that way today. Why should they? Well, Christ came into the world in order to set up one church, the same for everybody, but people decided to do things their own way."

"Well, perhaps it's simpler that way."

"Simpler..." Father Boris shook his head. "Simpler in some ways, perhaps. But remember, the Church is always one, it is only people that are evil. Take me, for example. I am the son of an uneducated mother. I was born in Leningrad, studied there in the seminary and Academy. Why do I, a simple person, understand Christ's commandment just as it is when he says, "Go ye into all the world, and preach the Gospel to every creature." Do you understand that? To every creature! To all the world. Not separately to Russians and Germans and Poles, not separately. People have gone badly wrong: the time has come to put everything back in place as Christ commanded. Or do you think he was looking for simple ways? He is truly patient, long suffering indeed, but how long can all this be allowed to go on? People think only of their own interests, but who is going to concern themselves with everything? People misunderstand me, they say I am proud! But I have passed beyond the seminarist's arrogance, I have overcome it, although now and again it manages to slip out. After all I, Father Boris, have been given a vocation. Do you understand what that means? Such visions have been revealed to me... But how could you possibly know what I am talking about?"

He plunged his big black velvety eyes deep into Skunk's

and made him feel very uneasy. The whole conversation was a bit weird and slightly scary. Father Boris was getting ever more excited, leaning too close to him, his breath hot on Skunk's face, their lips almost touching. Skunk moved back, pressing himself against the high back of the sofa, but the monk paid no heed to his uneasiness and continued to advance, as if not on him specifically but on some other person with whom he was prepared to argue until he was blue in the face. He talked on and on unwearyingly, some stuff about the Virgin Mary, some kind of light, the Pope, about how he understood them properly and other people didn't. He seemed almost to be on the verge of tears, but carried on disputing with his unseen opponent. Skunk suddenly felt very beside the point.

But Father Boris was getting more and more agitated, turned on by the sound of his own words. He seemed now to be addressing himself to the bolster on the sofa. His pupils narrowed and his eyes were fixed, almost unblinking, down there at one particular spot. Skunk became seriously alarmed. He wriggled out of the way, slipped off the sofa, and started getting his clothes back on. At first Father Boris did not understand what was happening and kept up his harangue, but suddenly, as if coming back to his senses, he broke off in mid-sentence.

"What are you doing? I hope you aren't frightened?"

"Nope. I have to go home now." Skunk had decided to make his excuses politely and leave.

"Don't even think of it. You are not going anywhere. Anyway, you don't have anywhere to go to. I could see that straight away. What are you doing? I am going to be your father and mother now. I am not unkind. Believe me, you will make me happy. There are two of us now. Just think of all the things we can do together." He was pleading, his eyes instantly brimming with affection; his face had grown long, and the bobbing cheeks had become sagging jowls.

Skunk immediately felt an emptiness in his heart. His body shook not with anger but with repulsion. Father Boris saw his trembling and returned to the fray with renewed vigour.

"Why are you trembling? What is it? You silly boy, surely you aren't afraid of me?" He reached out to Skunk, who jumped back. Father Boris sprang to his feet and barred the way.

"You can't do this, Daniil. It would not be Christian. Wait, my dear. You don't understand. I want to love you as a brother, as a father..."

At that Skunk's cup overflowed. He yelled in rage,

"Get off me, will you. Some Father you are, you crazy windbag. You can keep your Pope, it's time they sent you to the funny farm, you tin sledgehammer!"

"What are you saying, Daniil? You are ill, you are feverish. Wait! You don't understand. Just let me explain to you, let me teach you." Father Boris was by now a sorry sight, with his hairy paunch bulging out of his dressing gown, his legs with their white hair, his bare feet (at some point his slippers had come off), and his eyes those of a whipped cur.

"Daniil, Daniil, I beg you in the name of Christ our Saviour, stay. You don't understand. I, I, like a father..." He seemed suddenly to choke and, still trying to keep Skunk from leaving, unwisely reached out to him again. Skunk tore the blanket off the bed and threw it over his head. While he was floundering under it Skunk snatched up his jacket and the briefcase from the chair and ran outside to the porch.

For a long time, gradually calming down, he wandered along the bank beside the river until, shivering uncontrollably, he decided to risk going back home anyway; and there, in the warm, unnoticed by his mother, he sat in his corner on his bed until morning, staring fixedly ahead, and sucking his thumb.

15

His mother woke early. She had evidently had a skinful yesterday. She was shaking like a leaf, and her first act was reach
down for the beer she had prudently left under the bed to
relieve her hangover. No sooner had she started drinking from
it than a sinewy arm freed itself from under the blanket, pulled
the bottle from her lips, and emptied it down an insatiable
gullet surmounted by a black, thread-like moustache which
bristled beneath a nose the size of a pimple.

"You're a right one, Zoika." A small man so completely
covered in blue tattoos that it looked like body hair crawled
out from under the blanket, getting his breath back and belching.
Entirely unabashed by Skunk's presence, he jumped to his feet,
worked the muscles of his shoulders and abdomen and, fresh
and bare as a gherkin, stumbled barefoot to the bathroom.
Skunk's mother eyed his departing torso with open admiration,
then tried wretchedly to coax a last drop or two out of the
beer bottle and, catching Skunk's look of pure hatred, shouted
at him, "Wotcha staring at? Turn away and let a body get
dressed!"

Skunk fell back on to his pillow while she busied herself,
grunting and groaning, and finally waddled through to the
kitchen.

The tattooed man, draped now in a towel, leapt out of
the shower. He was as sturdy as a tree stump, with never an
ounce of fat on him and no suggestion of flabbiness or
lethargy. He glanced with a mischievous, self-satisfied grin
into Skunk's corner.

"Well now, young fellow, out steaming your fir cone till
midnight, were you?"

"Piss off!" Skunk put the over-familiar ones in their place
straight away.

"Wha-at? I didn't hear that. I did not hear that!" The
moustache quivered. "Say that again. You always that cheeky?

138

Didn't they teach you respect for your elders at school? Listen, you little snot-nose, you'd better watch your step. If it wasn't for mumsy here..." he snapped his fingers in front of Skunk's eyes. "Get the message? Now just you nip off round the corner smartish and get something to help with this hangover, right? And just remember, I don't say things twice. Zoika, haven't you got him trained or what?"

"Leave him be, Vlas. I'll go myself in a minute." His mother was standing in the doorway, and Skunk noticed real fear in her eyes.

"Leave him be?" The gangster (and that Vlas was a gangster had been clear from first glance) struck a pose and, holding his towel in place with one hand, raised the other in a Leninesque gesture and proclaimed, "You are advancing along the wight wood, comwades!" He suddenly cut himself short and barked viciously, "Get up! Get up now. I said you would go, and go you will, not her! Zoika!" He cut short the maternal urge to intercede, "Zoika, you understand me? I don't do jokes. I've had under age kids like this under my feet a wagon load and a trailer full as well, okay? He's going to run round there for us, he's not a glass prick, and bring back what we need, and then we can talk about it. You say he's screwing around? Forbidden sexual contacts? We'll soon beat that shit out of him, that clear?" He looked Skunk straight in the eyes. "I'm your daddy now, sonny, so just do as you're told, okay?"

Skunk got up obediently and pulled on his clothes. Vlas stood there flexing his muscles, watching, goading him with occasional phrases along the lines of "If you don't whip 'em you can't ride on 'em." When Skunk was ready he pointed his little finger at the bedside table.

"Poke around, sonny. There's dough in there. Get brandy, the best, something to eat with it, and sweeties for yourself while I'm in a good mood."

He turned away for an instant. Skunk had only a few seconds, and knew there wouldn't be another chance. He grabbed a heavy wooden stool, swung it with all his might, and brought it down from behind smack on the strutting rooster's head. It was a heavy blow. Vlas oinked, threw up his arms, and sank slowly to the floor. In order to give him no chance to recover, Skunk belted him a second and a third time with the stool, so hard that it came to pieces in his hand. Holding a leg of the stool in his hand like a cudgel he was about to finish him off when his mother rushed at him shrieking and knocked her son to the floor on top of her now inactive lover boy. Beside herself with rage, she seized Skunk by the hair with the evident intention of dragging him across the floor, but he tore free, leapt to his feet, and again raised the wooden bludgeon above his head and she re-directed her attention to her tattooed admirer. Blood was spurting from his battered head, a lot of blood, and the gangster was lying like a fish landed on the river bank with his eyes rolled up under his eyelids and giving no signs of life.

"You've killed him, you've killed him. Danny, you shit, have you really killed him? What have you done, Danny? You've killed him!"

His mother could not stop; wailing, she tore the wet towel from her hero's loins and tried to staunch the blood, but it kept flowing as if a tap had not been properly turned off. Then she rushed to the bathroom, brought a ladle of water, and poured it over her precious one and he stirred slightly, still unconscious, moving only his lips without opening his eyes. A moment later she at last managed to stop the bleeding and, having established that Vlas was not dead just yet, turned on Skunk who was still standing to one side, with the leg of the stool lowered but not yet abandoned.

"Do you know what you have done, you snake? Do you have any idea? For heaven's sake, this is Vlas: he's an authority. When he gets better he'll do you in. I mean, do you know what you have done, snake? Are you tired of life? Did you think of me, you snake, you slimy reptile? What life have I got

140

now? It'll be drudgery from now on. Where am I supposed to go? Where?" Her first shock had passed and she suddenly started howling, snivelling disgustingly, ageing in an instant. She lay there, crushed, disconsolate, finished, on the floor by the bare legs of her criminal lover, which were richly ornamented with a variety of images, symbols, and defiant underworld slogans.

"Why don't I just finish him off, mam?"

"Don't you dare, Danny, don't you dare!" His mother leapt to her feet, advancing on him. "Don't even think about it! Do you know what back-up he's got? Go away, go far, far away, to your woman, wherever you like, where you hid before. Go there. You won't live if you stay here after this." He could see the horror in her eyes; her hands were shaking. Her hair, all over the place, uncombed since she got out of bed, soaked in blood, fell over her face. She was beside herself, but Skunk knew that this time his mother was talking sense.

"Go away, I beg you in the name of all that's holy, go away. I'll look after myself somehow..." She started whimpering again, sank back down to the floor, turning her thug over on to his back, and started washing the blood out of his eyes.

"Go away, go away right now. God forbid his pals should come. Go away, Danny, I beg you..." She was still muttering the words when he made up his mind. He grabbed the rucksack, threw into it whatever came to hand, took his woodsman's fur jacket, hat and boots, and shovelled the money out of the priest's briefcase.

"I'll be off then, mam." He stood in the doorway and she nodded without looking up.

"God be with you, you snake, you reptile, you..."

"Mam..."

"Go away!" It was her last word, and she shrieked it so hysterically, so loudly, that he delayed no longer, closed the door, and went away.

16

It was still morning. The water truck had passed along the main street, but the sprayed asphalt wasn't yet steaming. Skunk headed for the station. He had decided straight away that if he had to hide anywhere then it might as well be in the forest, and the summer sun again called to mind his far off, elongated lake with its ducks and seagulls, the idiot wood grouse gobbling gravel, the unhurried clouds and forest humming with midges.

He felt no pangs of conscience. Quite the reverse, he regretted not having finished off that tattooed cretin. He was still incensed by him, and as for Valyusha or those pathetic monks, well, sod them all. His anger had guttered out. "The Lord helps those who help themselves" was the wide boys' motto. That seemed to be the way of the world now. As for the semi-poisonous, confusing things Father Boris had had to say: Catholics, Orthodox, what did it matter? He remembered his grandmother had been afraid of Catholics and thought you could expect nothing but dirty tricks from them; and her friends were all firmly convinced that the Antichrist would come from the Frankish lands, but who was he and what did he look like? Skunk didn't have room in his head for all that stuff. He didn't need that baggage. A good deal more disconcerting were his thoughts about his mother. What if Vlas, when he recovered, decided to take it out on her? But he persuaded himself that wouldn't happen: no, his mother would beguile him, billing and cooing all over him. She was always gentle and loving to these characters, and besides he, Skunk, was only a snake, and a slimy one at that. He was not happy to be walking like this through the town, down the main avenue to the railway station, past the opening newspaper kiosks, past people hurrying to the next shift, to their workbench, past the town's alkies who had crawled out to sun themselves. They were all unhurriedly enjoying their high, following him with their eyes, and sometimes sending an inoffensive enquiry after him, along the lines of, "Hey, lad, off fishing, then?" But he kept walking, his mouth clamped shut, the lips twisted to the side from tension. When he got to the station, when he had bought his ticket to the halt where, he hoped, his shotgun would still be safely buried, he hid behind the mail containers, sat out an hour or two examining the peeling surface of their corrugated sides, and emerged just before the train left, climbing into a top bunk. He spread out his jacket and instantly fell asleep.

He was being carried once more to the north. In his dreams he saw the fishermen accepting him into their team, and saw them working together. He was not afraid of hard work, he even longed for it. "Work heals everything," his grandmother used to say a long time ago. A long, long time ago.

Part Three

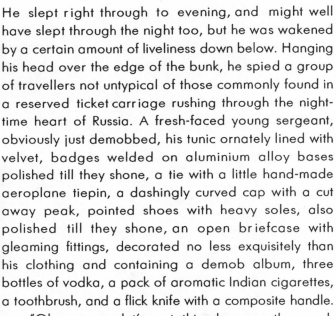

1

He slept right through to evening, and might well have slept through the night too, but he was wakened by a certain amount of liveliness down below. Hanging his head over the edge of the bunk, he spied a group of travellers not untypical of those commonly found in a reserved ticket carriage rushing through the night-time heart of Russia. A fresh-faced young sergeant, obviously just demobbed, his tunic ornately lined with velvet, badges welded on aluminium alloy bases polished till they shone, a tie with a little hand-made aeroplane tiepin, a dashingly curved cap with a cut away peak, pointed shoes with heavy soles, also polished till they shone, an open briefcase with gleaming fittings, decorated no less exquisitely than his clothing and containing a demob album, three bottles of vodka, a pack of aromatic Indian cigarettes, a toothbrush, and a flick knife with a composite handle.

"Okay, guys, let's get this show on the road. Help yourselves while I'm feeling generous," the young sergeant bared his gold-capped teeth at them. He was already well oiled and brimming with the milk of human kindness for everyone and everything in the world. Across from him on the lower bunk sat a puny lad wearing Montana jeans, a striped T-shirt with a zip, and a commander watch on his wrist, a with-it outfit manifestly at variance with his spotty physiognomy and lifeless fish eyes. This lad was viewing the bottles in the sergeant's case with some apprehension. Another passenger, of a kind often encountered on railway journeys and popularly and unkindly known as a deadbeat, was wearing a dirty, battered hat with a sagging brim. He had the weatherbeaten face of a professional beggar, filthy mitts, a canvas fitter's jacket, boots doubtless bought in a second- or thirdhand shop, and policemen's breeches of similar provenance. This personage, unlike fish eyes, was showing distinct interest in the contents of the case, and scratching a claw-like fingernail on the pull-down table, snivelling, and not allowing his lustful eyes to stray for a moment from the bottles.

"Join the party, guys. The army is celebrating. Here's to the demob order, sod it; here's to happiness at home, to the blue eyes waiting just for us!" The young sergeant waved his arm inclusively in the air, inviting everybody to join in; and of course there were soon more takers: two long-distance drivers, a grey little fisherman, and some other stray type; in no time people were producing bacon from the farm, cucumbers, sausage, salted fish, bread, and even a gallon can of warm beer with a very particular bitter smell. The sergeant was telling jokes tirelessly and, noticing Skunk's face up above, climbed up and specially invited him down.

"A hunter? Hey, great stuff. Where are you headed for? The taiga? What forests we have, brother: believe me or not, bears teeming like mice, two or three sitting there in every raspberry patch. You don't believe me? Never mind, come on down, brother, get some in you. It's what you need before you go off into the forest. Nobody's going to offer you one there, eh?" He burst out laughing in such a delightfully insolent way that to turn him down would have been the height of churlishness and quite unmanly. In order to avoid a chorus of condemnation, Skunk did come down and was soon sitting in the middle of their company, one of the group.

They were in the process of discussing the behaviour of the spotty youth skulking in the corner who was declining the proffered aluminium mug.

"No, I can't. I absolutely can't."

"Well why can't you? Did mumsy have you sideways, or did they find you under a gooseberry bush?"

"No, we can't." Here the boy assumed an appropriately solemn expression. "Warlocks aren't allowed to drink alcohol: it dissipates their energy."

"What's that again?" the assembled gathering gasped as one.

"I've got a Korean teacher in Moscow, you know," the boy elaborated. "He's a real Korean from Korea, not a Soviet one. He came to Russia about two years back and now he's a lecturer at the Academy of Paranormal Phenomena."

"Paranormal? Flying saucers and all that?" one of the drivers asked.

"Well, yes, they are working on flying saucers too, only that's a different section, but our section is manual therapy and acupuncture, healing through laying on of hands, and needles."

"Needles, tee-hee," the tramp sniggered. "How does that work?"

"What, don't you know?" the young sergeant stood up for the boy. "They stick them in your nerve centres and relieve stress and rheumatism."

"Can you do that? Cure rheumatism?"

"Rheumatism's a piece of piss," the lad said, plainly enjoying being the centre of attention. "Our teacher treats cancer, radiation sickness, sterility. He can even call down rain."

"How's that?" the sergeant asked puzzled.

"Oh, even my grandad can do that. I started learning from him, you know, and went to Moscow afterwards. We have to purify ourselves for a long time first, accumulating energy, and afterwards you're allowed to release it, but not all of it, or you might die."

"That's clear enough. Like a battery," the driver interjected,

146

and poured everyone another vodka. "So, you aren't allowed to do anything, you live on grass and nuts accumulating energy. Er, what about women, while we're on the subject?"

The boy went crimson and at first huffily said nothing, but then, unable to contain himself, muttered under his breath, but actually for the benefit of Skunk, who was sitting next to him, "He thinks he's getting at me, the moron, but I could put the evil eye on him."

His threat was drowned in a clattering of glasses, and no sooner was that round over than another was poured. Skunk, hardly noticing how it happened, suddenly found himself one of the boys. At least he did not want to be like this half-baked warlock. Very soon the sergeant was waving a wad of banknotes in the air. He theatrically tore off the label and disappeared for a moment, returning in no time at all with four new bottles and two young women who shrieked and giggled affectedly. Everyone moved up to squeeze them into the circle, and wholeheartedly set about the task of getting them drinks and finding them something to eat. The celebration took off. One minute the carriage would be full of unfamiliar newcomers, the next unexpectedly empty. Somebody, naturally, was snoring in one of the bunks, somebody else bringing more bottles. Like all self-respecting passengers they got the carriage attendant drunk, and one of the drivers went off with her to her compartment, clutching the air more often than he clutched the guffawing attendant, and they locked themselves in and left the drinkers to get on with their celebrating without due official supervision.

At some point Skunk must have passed out, because when he returned to the land of the living he discovered the warlock sitting in the corner whispering to one of the girls who was, alas, openly yawning and constantly asking him, "But what about the money? I suppose they do pay you lots of money?"

"Why else would I be doing it? Only, you know what, this money of mine has got a hex on it. It's unnickable. Look!" He pulled a pouch from inside his shirt and, hiding it from everyone else, showed only her what it had inside.

"Wow!" The girl finally showed a bit of interest. Skunk noticed that at that moment the deadbeat too gave the moneybag a sharp glance, but immediately turned away again, leaned over against the sergeant and appeared to start snoring. The sergeant meanwhile was touching up the other girl. He had the album with his photos of life in the army out on his knees and was explaining some crucial detail to her, trying in the process to get his arm round her and pull her closer. The young lady was quite properly pushing his arm off, but nevertheless looking in the album wide eyed, and clearly very taken by everything she saw there. Most of the partygoers and people from practically the whole of the rest of the carriage had drifted away by now. Skunk dozed off again, only to be wakened by the young sergeant shaking him insistently by the shoulder. The old deadbeat was no longer there, having presumably got off, and neither were the affected girls; only the somnolent warlock, who was looking cross about something, was peering red-eyed out of his corner.

"Wake up, Danny, wake up. Let's have a last drink. I have to get out soon." The sergeant could barely stand upright, but he was just as amiable and happy as before they had started.

"Come on, Danny. This spider is no friend of ours. He's too busy accumulating energy. Isn't that right?" The sergeant snapped his fingers in front of the warlock's nose. "What you looking so glum about? Didn't you get it up? Oh, Danny," he sniggered. "You should have seen him working on Lenka, but when it was time for her to get off, she really told him where he could get off. You really got on her tits, pal. Still, never mind. Save up all your energy, and if your left hand gets tired your right can take over, eh?"

The offended warlock turned his face to the wall and feigned sleep, and the sergeant, instantly forgetting him, set to work on Skunk again.

148

"Come on, Danny. There's still some vodka in carriage five. I'll just run and get some. It's Glubinka in half an hour: that's my stop. I'll have to get out. Fancy another?" He stuck his hand into his pocket, then into a different one, then started rummaging through his little case.

"God knows where it is. We can't have drunk our way through three thousand." His expression became worried and even guilty. "My brother sent me it so I could come home in style. Now it looks like someone's nicked it."

"Perhaps you shouldn't have waved it about quite so much," Skunk blurted out unkindly. "Look again and see if you haven't put it somewhere."

A further search proved equally fruitless.

"Here, you! Listen," an idea suddenly occurred to the sergeant and he turned on the warlock. "I don't suppose you saw anything, did you?"

"No," he replied unwillingly and shut his eyes again.

"Hang on! Where's that old tramp? That deadbeat in the hat? He was supposed to be staying on to Arkhangelsk, so he said."

"He got off at Pustoy Bor," the warlock responded from his corner.

"There! I might have known it. I can't stand these freeloaders. I bet it was him that nicked it. What am I to do now? How am I going to get home?" The lad was quite crestfallen and had suddenly sobered up.

"Oh dearie, dearie me!" Skunk suddenly made his mind up. He climbed up to his bunk, pulled his jacket from under somebody who was asleep up there, and pulled out of an inner pocket a package wrapped in cloth. "Here," he said, handing it to the sergeant. "It's all yours."

"Are you crazy?"

"What use is it to me? Am I supposed to salt it for the winter? I won't need money in the forest, and if we meet up some time you can give it me back."

149

"Danny, do you really mean it?" The sergeant cheered up instantly. "Look, the minute I get home I'll go straight to the transport depot. I can make piles of money there. Hey, why don't you come with me? You've no idea what the hunting's like. I'll introduce you to a hunter, he's my godfather, how about it?"

"No, just take it."

"Listen, Danny, I mean it. Come with me!"

But Skunk only shook his head. The train started losing speed, and the young sergeant had to get a move on collecting his modest belongings together. He scribbled his address on a scrap of paper, noted down Skunk's, and swore he would send the money in a month or two. Then he started hugging him, urging him all the while to come with him. "Glubinka may mean out in the sticks, but it's not really that bad. Ask for Valka Shornikov, they all know me. You will look me up, won't you now, good buddy? You damn well better, or I'll come looking for you myself, and then it'll be curtains. And I will come. Expect me. The girls were from Stargorod, I've got their address. I'll be on a plane there sooner or later, you'll see. Well, put it there, pal, and take it easy. It's a deal, as soon as you get back from the forest I'll be there, agreed?"

"Sure. See you then." Skunk couldn't think how to get rid of him.

The boisterous sergeant finally disappeared into the corridor, but then stood outside the window, hammering his fist on it and shouting until the train glided out.

"The old man took the money off him. I saw him do it," the warlock suddenly reported from his corner.

"What do you say I cut you up right now, you shit?" Skunk suddenly asked in his best gangland accent.

"No chance, I can see through people. You gave that money away, so you're on the same wavelength as the soldier, one of God's own. People don't earn money by the sweat of their brow just to blow it like that." The warlock was obviously scared, but even so couldn't keep his mouth shut. Skunk was impressed.

"Well just you listen, you stinking goat, you ought to be swatted like a fly, but to hell with you. Carry right on accumulating your money."

He fell on to his bunk and turned to the wall, but did not sleep despite being well and truly pissed. It was the first time, he supposed, that he had been this plastered, and hearing the pimply warlock mumbling something to himself, he felt a sudden surge of incredible happiness and lightness. He had finally got rid of that money, and was once more as pure and innocent as in earliest childhood.

2

He arrived at his halt towards the end of the following day. In the pallid twilight of a sub-arctic summer's night he sought out the place and dug up the shotgun and ammunition. He had greased it lavishly, and tucked it up more lovingly than if it had been a newborn babe, and it was as good as new. He struck off into the forest, put five miles or so between him and the nearest human habitation, lit a fire, and set to cleaning the grease off the shotgun. He had more than enough gunpowder, pellets and bullets. Vitaly had left him a rich legacy and now, as he readied the gun, he remembered that winter, the hunter, his fears and the illness which had suddenly come upon him, and equally suddenly lifted. This time, he hoped, things would be different. Just as before he was not afraid of isolation but, having grown up a little, and knowing a bit more about survival in the forest, recognized that it would be no bad thing to find himself a companion. He was wagering on the fishermen being there. His instinct, which so far had not let him down, told him that was how it would be. That he would be accepted into the team he did not doubt. People were a resource in short supply in the forest.

June was coming to an end, the game birds were still teaching elementary skills to their fledglings, and he vowed that as far as possible he would kill only the males, since these had already performed their main function, although, as they were now moulting, they skulked in obscure hiding places. Even this was all to the good: he would have to run a bit harder to winkle them out. The hunting itch was beginning get to him again and his ears, which had so often lacked employment in the city, now picked up the slightest sound or rustle.

Skunk was in no hurry. At the halt he had bought bread and flour, salt, matches, and vinegar essence for the skins, and virtually drained his financial resources in the process: his own money, of course, not the priest's. On a metal sheet he had picked up along the way specially for the purpose he dried out the bread over the fire.

In the nearest stream he guddled some fish, and that was his supper at this involuntary stop. When he had all his preparations complete, he got himself ready for good and earnest, packed up his rucksack and set forth to the north. He walked and walked and walked, not in last year's fraught and desolate frame of mind, but with the composure of a seasoned woodsman.

The heat was beyond belief. There had been no rain for a long time. The air in the forest was stifling; the bogs were steaming and many had even dried up. In the woods pine needles rustled under foot like paper, and for now the dominant smell of resin overpowered all others. In the dry, windless forest the one terrible power which he did fear was fire. He kept his campfires very small, and went to great lengths to douse and stamp them out before moving on. The jays and ravens often followed in his wake, broadcasting to all the inhabitants of the forest that man was approaching, but he was making no attempt to hide. He strode along confidently, only shooting a stupid hazel grouse for food when one invited him to. He calculated that he still had one or two days' march to go. He was already beginning to recognize his surroundings: a long yellow bog, not dangerous (he walked straight through the middle of it); a lake like a saucer, a slightly larger one with a small island in the middle. He was almost at journey's end. Time and freedom again became endless, his and his alone, and Skunk looked round eyed about him to every side, joyfully registering the squeaking of the squirrels, the chirr of mother hazel grouse calling her brood to her, and catching the heavy beating of wings as some fattening wood grouse took to the air.

He came to yet another small lake, broke off plenty of young fir branches, and made himself one last bed in the open air. He lit a fire, roasted hazel grouse in the embers, and gazed at the sky and the slow, almost motionless clouds. He felt at home here, and now could not imagine how any power could have driven him away, or why he should ever have gone back to the city. That there had been such a power he remembered well: he could feel it even now, and talked to it. About nothing. About something.

3

Skunk woke in the middle of the night: never in his life had he sensed so much alarm positively spilling out all around him. A grey, sullen sky flecked with lead, a strange oppressive heat; the smell in the air was not the usual resinous smell, but had something else mixed in with it, and a haze hung over the distant forest. He very soon guessed that this was no haze: far off in the region of his lake a forest fire was raging. Smoke enveloped the horizon and rose to the sky, mingling with the grey night air; his nostrils were beginning to detect the thin smell of burning. He needed to move away speedily, but where to? He climbed up a tall fir tree and from the top could see only billowing clouds of smoke. The whole of the north, east

153

and west was in flames and the fire was evidently headed his way, since he suddenly noticed a herd of deer running across the bog straight at him, towards the south.

Up in his treetop a breeze was playing, a northerly breeze which was gradually freshening and, knowing these parts, Skunk supposed that towards morning the wind would strengthen and the fire would travel faster.

He climbed down and conscientiously stamped out his fire. He decided to flee back to the lake with the small island in the middle where he would have nothing to fear from the fire. For the rest of the night he strode rapidly, almost running, through pine woods, over bogs, and was often outflanked by birds flying in panic. Every inhabitant of the forest without exception was making a run for it; all around the woods were rustling with the sound of hooves and claws, and the air was full of the beating of wings. The fire was evidently close on his heels.

The wind did indeed strengthen, and now the smell of burning and burnt resin was unmistakable and he began to run. He ran headlong, over tussocks and into hollows, stumbling and jumping up again, himself seized by the panic of the natural world.

In front there loomed the long large swamp, and in the middle of it he suddenly noticed a gigantic elk. In his fear the beast seemed even greater than the one last year. The elk was resting, half turned towards the north and the advancing wall of fire, and towards Skunk who was running straight at it. Its nostrils were flaring furiously: evidently it had been running for a long time; and its intelligent, sad eyes seemed to be looking straight at the man. Skunk reloaded his gun, slammed in a bullet cartridge, shoved a second in his pocket, and rushed into the open space yelling. The elk quivered, tensed, and soundlessly melted away on its long legs into the depths of the forest. He too seemed to be heading for the lake; at all events Skunk made haste to follow him and soon came out to another clearing, another swamp, in the centre of which lay the lake which promised salvation. He raced blindly towards it and, turning to look back, saw the smoke less than half a mile away. When he had almost reached the shore he realized to his horror that his plan was doomed. The tussocky bog more or less supported a man's weight, but as he approached the water it became ever more dangerous. He was already beginning to sink knee-deep, even up to his waist, and by the water's edge there was an impassable quagmire which completely cut off the island sanctuary and its thin, twisted little pine trees. For all that, there was a lot of water here, too much indeed, and he eventually fell down on to a mound of some sort in order to get his breath back. He was completely worn out, and lay face down on the dry, prickly sedge grass, dirty, half soaked, and only then spread his jacket, leaning against his rucksack, and thus, more or less established on his tiny patch of land, turned to face the advancing fire.

First came the smoke. It spread over the ground, wisps flying like torn rags through the air, and was soon billowing at him as if out of a chimney. He could scarcely see the pines and firs in the forest. Suddenly, as if by magic, the smoke vanished. Skunk heard the crackling of flames and spied the strip of fire. It was running along the ground, through the pine needles, like an endlessly writhing fox's tail. He watched this ground fire entranced as it raced along merry and insatiable, the way the fire had raced over poplar down which the children set fire to in the streets of the city in June when he was a child: an orange-yellow, harmless looking serpent. Now it had slithered across the ravine and crept into the pine grove from which he had leapt out to the swamp in the tracks of the elk; and suddenly, in an inexpressibly fast moment, the fire spread, spiralling upwards and exploding and... for a few instants the trees stood unscathed like the biblical burning bush, surrounded by haloes of raging flame, but, unable to withstand the searing heat, their crowns burst into flame like candles from hell, sparks flying upwards into the heavens; and then the wind bent the flames and drove the fire on past Skunk in his marshy refuge.

It was too soon to say it had gone past. Certainly the wall of flame had swept on past the bog and was lapping at the next pine wood. It had rushed by like a river, but the forest fire proper was only now getting under way. The trees were still ablaze, but now giving off acrid smoke, and all about was instantly covered in black soot and ashes. The unbearably hot air made Skunk press himself down into his tussock to where the water was seeping up, but this was not much help. The fire was everywhere. The sedge was burning and sparking, his jacket and clothing began to smoulder, and then Skunk hauled the billy can out of his rucksack and started bailing the dirty bog water over himself from head to foot. The can filled painfully slowly. Skunk crawled around his little haven of territory and over the slurping, treacherous marsh, beyond fear, searching for hollows, bailing the water out of them, drenching himself, but the water evaporated immediately. The smoke was suffocating and he was on the verge of passing out.

At some point Skunk looked over towards the lake and, wonder of wonders, there on the little island stood the giant elk. It stood with its head bent to the ground, and seemed to be observing his frantic efforts. How had it got there? Had it come round from the other side, or did it know a path through the marsh? One thing was clear, out there, surrounded by water, was a much more comfortable and safer place to be, and Skunk was duly envious.

He continued crawling about in this manner for another one and a half or two hours, because the first wave of fire was followed by a second which devoured anything left untouched by the first, and in its wake came sparks and tongues of flame, licking and finally finishing off anything that was still alive.

The fire burned all day and all night and Skunk, absolutely exhausted, would at one moment sink down on his mound, to be impelled almost immediately by the heat to crawl again in circles; and only towards evening when the hellfire had moved on did he collapse on to his much crawled over refuge and fall into a deep sleep. The last thing he noticed was the elk, now standing erect and looking, as before, directly at him.

4

It was time to get up and go on, but where to? To his lake? To the fishermen's camp? That would mean walking over blackened ground which was still lit up here and there by sparks from little conflagrations. Perhaps he should strike out eastwards? He did not know the extent of the disaster; the whole area around him was black and smoking, and totally lifeless; hot cinders rustled underfoot; but, with characteristic stubbornness, Skunk nevertheless decided to carry on straight ahead. After all, he tried to convince himself, the fishermen's hut was located on a lakeside clearing where the trees had been rooted out, on space won from the forest, and the fire might have spared it. In any case, what option did he have? It was the only place he knew, apart from that triangle he had tramped so many times last year with Vitaly. So now, secretly calling upon his forest guardian angel, he persuaded himself that one of the three huts must have survived and would be waiting there for him; and even if the fishermen were not back, he would at least have somewhere to sit out the bad times.

He walked through a place which only yesterday had been alive, but today was destroyed and destined not to recover for many long years to come. The usual sounds and smells had gone, and he trailed behind him a cloud of dust and ashes, hardly looking about him, advancing dully like a machine programmed to follow a strict compass bearing. Even the ubiquitous midges had been blown away and incinerated. Only in the smoking piles of the anthills was life already beginning to break through again. Having taken shelter deep in their underground hives, tireless as a force of nature, the insects were now scurrying over the heaps of earth, squirting their corrosive secretions on the smouldering sparks, often perishing in the process, but nevertheless succeeding in putting out the flames with their invisible droplets. Apart from the ants no movement presented itself to the eye. Only his footsteps rustled loudly in the silence.

As he walked he munched his dried bread, ate a sugar cube, and drank it all down with water from the swamp. He did not want to risk stopping for a rest, anxious to conserve his meagre supply of provisions. In the evening, as black as a chimney sweep, he emerged on to the shore of his lake. The mother ducks were bobbing on the water: they had not abandoned their unfledged ducklings; but he saw no sign of the seagulls and swans. He promptly shot two scrawny goldeneye ducks: one was carried far away by the current, but he managed to get hold of the second, and was thereby assured of supper.

After that he walked another half mile round the shore. On the familiar mound all was chaos. Alas, the fire had got the house and the shed with the boats; of course it had burned down the bathhouse too, and spared only the lean-to by the water's edge with the fish gutting dug-out. All the habitable buildings were totally ruined. There was not a soul to be seen: the team had not returned for the fishing. He rearranged some of the blackened barrels and settled down in the lean-to, roasted the duck he had killed and devoured it whole, he was that hungry. Only then did he wander over to the burned out remains of the house. He found the hatchet there and the axe with their handles charred, bowls with a hole burned in their enamel, a flattened bucket. The boats had dried out and were charred, the nets had gone up in the flames. He sat down on a boulder on the shore and stared at the opposite bank. It was burned out too, and soundless. He sat there all night, motionless, gazing vacantly into the black mirror of the water.

Towards morning when sleep finally overcame him, through

his swollen heavy eyelids he imagined he saw the elk again. It seemed to be keeping an eye on him, concealing itself there on the other shore between the big pine trees. He was going to force himself to get up in order to move under the covering, but then saw quite unmistakably the live, hunch-backed figure of the animal and sleep was banished instantly. Skunk gave a loud, hoarse yell, startling the beast. It went off into the forest but soon reappeared, closer, perhaps a quarter of a mile away, inspecting the lonely, frightened man.

He could only assume that the beast was pursuing him for its own dark reasons, so, as he always did before a risky undertaking, Skunk once more prepared himself mentally and counted his ammunition once again: five bullets, more than enough. He accepted the challenge. Here, on the devastated shores of this lake, there was no more to be done. Once again the thrill of the chase took possession of him, depriving him of his usual clear thinking. He got to his feet and moved off straight towards the beast. The elk tossed its head and vanished among the trees. The hunt was on.

5

Skunk did not know much about the habits of the bull of the forests. He knew from Vitaly's tales that they were particularly dangerous in September when they were pursuing, courting, and covering the does.

But this was June. There was no Vitaly beside him and nobody to explain the peculiar behaviour of the beast. Why, when it got too far away from him, did the elk stop as if it was waiting specially for him to catch up? The bull did not try to circle round and come upon him from behind. Instead, it led him steadily towards the north east, apparently heading for the mysterious land of Koloch about which Skunk had heard so many legends.

They tramped on for a day, then another, and another

and another. The burned out forest had long since been left behind and in the damp bogs the beast's tracks were clearly visible. Where the ground was dry he seemed to be specially marking his progress, leaving hoof prints and not changing direction, making it impossible to lose track of him. On top of that, several times a day the elk would show itself to Skunk, not allowing him within range for a shot, but also having no apparent inclination to attack him.

Skunk's nerves were stretched to the limit. He slept fitfully when he could and, totally worn out, on the third or fourth day of the pursuit, climbed up into a tree, made himself a resting place, and there in its branches slept to his heart's content. He had almost no doubt that the beast was leading him to some destination. His meagre food supply came to an end and, as he was walking along, he picked off a large wood grouse in a fir tree. What kind of beast was it that did not run away when it heard a shot, even thought it knew it was being pursued? But the giant bull looked over from the far side of a bog, satisfied its curiosity, disappeared into the thickets, and stood there through the night, not far away, waiting.

Skunk lost the urge to hunt. If he had found the elk right next to him, he probably would have fired at it in fright, but not as a hunter; and quite possibly he would not have shot even so. The beast instilled in him a tremor almost of awe.

So they carried on for two more days. The forest began to change. Increasingly now they encountered bogs with dangerous quagmires, the surface covered over with weed and duckweed. Here Skunk trod in the steps of his long-legged guide. He supposed they must already have crossed over into Koloch: lumps of cliff rose up out of the ground here. These were not glacial boulders grey with lichen, however, but bare rock, with occasional bushes of creeping dogrose, and tufted with eyebrows of dry grass.

The elk changed its tactics. Now it remained visible almost all the time. Skunk looked constantly at its great hulk, glimpsed through the trees, or else in a vast swamp he watched how confidently the huge animal, obviously knowing where it was going, picked its way through terrifying mire. At times it would forge straight ahead, at others loop and circle, avoiding deadly marshes.

And then in front of him an enormous swamp extended as far as the eye could see, a whole world in itself, several miles in extent, with little islands and lakes and rivulets. Beyond it rose a forest and high cliffs, the size of a good five-storey building. The elk increased its pace: Skunk, however, slowed down almost to a crawl. The marsh to either side was very frightening, and on top of that he suddenly remembered Vitaly's tales of radiation. He reasoned, however, that if beasts could inhabit Koloch, then he should come to little harm himself. And even geologists, apparently, came here to work. This was a talking swamp: at one moment to one side it would sigh, loudly sucking in air; it would gurgle and slurp or, on the contrary, hiss as it released an accumulation of gas. Skunk furiously prodded in front of himself with a staff, and sometimes the pole would disappear into brackish water, and he would freeze in terror, but then he would seek out a firm tussock and step on that.

The marsh sapped all his remaining strength. The elk had long since disappeared in the forest, but Skunk was still crawling forward, and the closer he got to salvation, the more he was beset by weariness. There was no place here he could sit down to rest, and like it or not he had to keep moving.

And then disaster struck. Some three hundred yards from dry land, in a place over which the elk had passed, in a place where his staff had promised him a safe foothold, the marsh suddenly opened up with a sigh and Skunk was sucked in. His legs were trapped. Knowing the danger of any sudden movement, he threw his staff cross-wise, tore the rucksack from his shoulders and tucked it under his chest, and for a time that held him. But then slowly, very slowly, driving bubbles out of the filthy water, he began to sink; and then, looking straight at the burning sun, Skunk fired a shot in the air, fully aware of the futility of the gesture. Then he struggled with all his strength to pull himself out, but only got stuck more firmly. There was no one he could look to for salvation. He was overcome by terror, and started struggling and yelling, sensing the imminence of death.

But then he heard an answering human shout. He thought he must be hearing things, but suddenly saw that a peculiar looking man was rushing towards him from the edge of the swamp. He was clad in a black robe and carrying a long staff. The man was running like a hare, leaping from tussock to tussock. Skunk saw only a long beard and matted locks of hair; he reached out his arms and seized hold of the staff extended towards him.

He did not remember how they both got out of the swamp. It seemed to him that the man with the beard was singing something familiar, perhaps even something he had heard in church. He realized that he really must be going mad. His saviour fairly dragged him to the shore, and when he once again had solid ground beneath his feet, Skunk, still clutching the staff, plunged headlong into oblivion.

6

When he came to he was lying in a clearing or, more exactly, a barren area enclosed on three sides by cliffs and on the fourth by a thin wood through which the fearsome marsh glimmered. He was wrapped in a thick woven blanket, his head resting on a specially bevelled block of wood. A long-haired man clad in a long home-made garment which most closely resembled a worn-out cassock was kneeling beside him deep in prayer. His hands were pressed together on his chest, his eyes closed, and he seemed oblivious to his surroundings, so intent and austere was the expression on his lean face; but the moment Skunk shifted, his saviour opened his eyes, cast a rather wild glance at him, and made a broad sign of the Cross over himself.

"Glory be to our Lord Jesus Christ now and forever more, amen!" he proclaimed in a loud voice and, skipping lightly to his feet, hung over the newly conscious Skunk.

"Lie still, lie still!" the strange person commanded him peremptorily but not threateningly, the strict expression on his ageing face lit up with a smile.

"There now, you have come at last! I have been waiting for you for such a long time. God is merciful, he has remembered me, unworthy as I am," he added quietly.

Then he filled a ladle from a bucket standing on the ground:

"Drink some of this infusion of cranberries. It will bring you back to earth in an instant."

Skunk drank it down mechanically, quailing at the incredible sourness, but said nothing and gazed in amazement at the stranger.

"Well, well, there is nothing in this world of sin that cannot be explained. Caesar is my tame elk. He evidently decided to play a little game, and brought you here. Wake up, wake up. You are alive and well, and whatever the Lord contrives is for the best!" The man's jocularity was plainly well meant: he wanted to make himself agreeable. "Are you a hunter? Where are your dogs?"

"..."

"Fine. Oh, by the way, your gun and rucksack sank, but we'll find some clothes for you to wear, and you won't be needing a gun here. Settle in, make yourself at home, and welcome to the hermitage."

He moved away, leaving Skunk alone, in order to give him a chance to collect his thoughts. So there really was nothing all that miraculous about it all. A tame elk... Skunk looked up at the sky. He did not even want to move. The blanket had warmed him and he would quite surely have fallen asleep, but

163

the man in the robe returned bringing a kettle of tea and now calmly, over the tea, told him his story.

This place had been given to Father Innokenty in answer to his prayers. He had found himself here by a miracle, having lost his way in a blizzard one winter. He had slept at first in the geologists' abandoned cabin, eating his way through their remaining supplies. Later he had constructed a hut, a separate chapel, knocked together a bathhouse, and lived here happily with God's blessing. Only the following winter had he sought out human company, got himself supplies of vegetables, seeds, and a fishing net, and dragged everything to his hermitage on a sleigh. Come the spring he made himself a vegetable garden. He caught fish in a nearby lake, and gathered mushrooms and berries in the woods. Nothing out of the ordinary, he seemed to think, and he told the tale laconically, undramatically. Skunk trusted him.

For two days, while Skunk was coming to his senses, Father Innokenty left him to his own devices. He settled him in the old cabin, and came in only to call him for meals. Skunk ate himself to a standstill. For the first time in many days he supped hot soup, drank rose hip tea, and slept for as long as he liked. The monk did not trouble him with unwanted questions, and heated up the bathhouse. Skunk had a good wash and scraped off all the grime. By the morning of the third day he was his old self again.

He woke early, before sunrise; in effect it was still night. He came out to the clearing. Father Innokenty was apparently still asleep. The monk went to bed late, and before retiring prayed at length in the chapel. Fearing to disturb him, Skunk went off to the lake, found a rough hewn aspen canoe on the shore, checked out the nets, gutted the catch, put a can of water on the fire, and only when the water had boiled did he see the monk emerging from the chapel. He had got up even earlier to pray in his accustomed solitude.

They made fish soup, a standard item on the hermitage's

menu, and Father Innokenty said grace. The monk ate a lot, but mindfully, as if laying up a store of energy, then said another grace in conclusion, and joyously noticing that Skunk had, in some embarrassment, made the sign of the Cross on his forehead, asked, "Have you been christened?"

Receiving an affirmative answer, he nodded to him. Then they worked together in the vegetable garden, weeding the beds. Then they sawed firewood until evening, hardly speaking. The monk was silent, giving an occasional instruction or replying to a practical question from Skunk.

Towards evening they lit a fire, boiled some potatoes, heated up the remains of the soup and had their supper. Father Innokenty again said grace briefly before and after the repast. Then he got up and quietly disappeared into the chapel, leaving the boy alone.

So it continued for several days. Having first shown how happy he was to have company, the monk made no further show of joy, and Skunk realized he was being tested. Taciturn since birth, he had no trouble passing this examination and assumed responsibility, with the incumbent's consent, for doing the cooking, cleaning the pots, and watching the nets. He suggested to the monk that they should build an ice house, dug it out himself, reinforced the walls with an aspen pallisade, made a roof to cover it, and buried it in earth. He salted away surplus fish in a specially allocated barrel. In short, he resumed last year's familiar way of life. He would work during the day, the monk sometimes helping him, and in the evenings he would sit out on the steps of the cabin or beside the fire, drinking tea and enjoying the silence. Thus one week passed and another. Father Innokenty would disappear for most of the time into the chapel but Skunk, not having been invited, did not look in there, and only called him to meals.

As he had been that first moment, Father Innokenty was invariably kind and considerate, but he did not enter into lengthy conversations and, emerging from the chapel, seemed embarrassed, as if feeling that here was Skunk working hard while he was wasting time.

Thus their first month passed.

7

Koloch proved to be quite an amazing place. Only this tiny patch of land had been wrested by man from nature. Ten paces in any direction saw the beginning of virgin countryside. In the forest there were not even any cuts on the trees to indicate routes. The animals roamed free, but wild or tame, they were all drawn to the monk. There was, for instance, a pair of ravens: officious and inquisitive, they often circled nearby, and would seize fish right out of your hand or, if their provider was not around, summon him with impatient, raucous cries. Caesar also came, but less often than the ravens. He would appear unannounced and depart equally unexpectedly. He would lick the salt left out for him or accept a boiled potato, carefully and graciously picking every last crumb of the gift from the hand of the monk with his lips; but he did not allow Skunk to come near: he would snort and roll his eyes. The monk would whisper something soothing, stroke the beast's mighty back, scratch behind its ear, and the bull would half close its eyes, trembling slightly with pleasure and emitting infrequent but singularly un-elklike sounds.

Towards the end of July the first mushrooms appeared and agreeably enlivened the meals in the hermitage. Father Innokenty now often went off into the forest. One time, when the monk was off mushroom gathering, Skunk, unable to contain his curiosity, glanced into the chapel. It was dark and cool in the simple little building, or more precisely cabin, built directly on the earth without even a wooden floor. Instead of panes in the windows there were planks: two little arrow slits in the log walls. He took them down and light flooded in, instantly blending with the darkness to produce a restful half-light. On a bench by the wall lay a jar with candle ends and a box of matches. Directly opposite the door, on the log wall, hung cheap icons of the Saviour, the Mother of God, and St Nicholas. Slightly higher there was a cardboard icon of the Trinity, and beneath that an icon lamp. The wick was not lit. Father Innokenty was evidently economizing on oil.

Skunk closed the door and sat down on the bench. There was a fragrance of resin, wax, and the clinging smell of burnt oil. He closed his eyes, immersing himself in the stillness. When the door opened and Father Innokenty appeared in the doorway, Skunk calmly raised his eyes. He did not feel any guilt at his intrusion. The monk, appreciating his mood, nodded affirmatively, closed the door tight, went over to the iconostasis, lit the icon lamp and began to read the hours.

His reading was unhurried, accomplished, and beautiful, in the monastic manner, pronouncing each word clearly, with that slight but noticeable sing-song which draws you after it without in any way jarring as fussy church services often do with the wailing and crowing of the readers and deacons. Skunk rose from the bench: it didn't seem right, and in any case he no longer felt like sitting. He positioned himself back a little beside the door, and began unexpectedly to chant the familiar: "Come, let us bow and fall down before the Lord Jesus Christ our God". Having begun there was no stopping. "Give ear to my words, O Lord, considering my meditation." Slowly and smoothly they voyaged through the fifth psalm. Where Skunk did not remember he fell silent, what he knew he chanted easily and earnestly: "For thou, Lord, wilt bless the righteous man; with favour wilt thou compass him as with a shield"; and the prayer to the Mother of God; and like a counting off of the rosary, taking its lead from the chanting, forty times Father Innokenty intoned, "Lord have mercy" and Skunk responded. After all the silence the prayers were soothing and pleasant, and it was long before the last one came to an end: "Christ, true light of the world", and the conclusive "Amen!"

167

Father Innokenty turned towards him and repeated those first words of his, but with a different, more profound and heartfelt intonation: "You have come, my son!" And straight away, in the same breath, he asked sharply and severely: "Do you desire confession?"

Skunk nodded in fright.

The monk went out and returned with a crucifix, a Bible, and vested in his priestly stole. First he prayed for a long time. Rather too long, it seemed: Skunk grew tired of waiting. Then the monk put the stole over Skunk's bowed head and listened, only occasionally prompting him: "Speak, speak, my son!"

8

A solid bond of trust was established between them. To tell the truth, all the hard work added welcome variety. There was more to be done than could be fitted into twenty-four hours, and Father Innokenty released Skunk from the early morning vigil for which he himself now got up without fail. He had greatly missed the long monastery services. When alone he had not been able to afford the time to observe the monastic routine and now, hungry, spent longer on the services, delegating the domestic duties to his unexpected companion.

The monk was forthright. He didn't affect spurious strictness or a didactic tone, and if he found Skunk gazing at him meditatively he would shout mischievously: "What are you staring at? A monk is just a human being, only more sinful than any other!"

He seemed not so much to instruct as to be sharing his thoughts with an equal, but he recollected Skunk's life in every detail and often in the evenings by the fire over supper, as if in passing, would return to some episode, slightly prompting him, and again Skunk would talk and talk, bringing every last thing out into the open.

So they lived, readying supplies for the winter, the main

test of the year, when the monk would go into the world, to a village which reliably and secretly kept the recluse supplied with provisions for the coming months.

"Without them I should long since be in my grave," Father Innokenty once admitted. "It seems you can't get by without relying on the world. It has taken me some time to understand that."

He settled himself comfortably, poured himself out some tea from the kettle, and Skunk prepared to listen: the monk was obviously about to embark upon a topic he considered important.

"Well now, do you think I ran off here from love of the Lord?" He winked conspiratorially. "No, young fellow, I wanted a breath of freedom. I had lived in the world, I had seen people, bureaucrats and bosses, the way the fat cats lived, and there was no place for me there.

I went off to the seminary, and later to a monastery. I was at ease there and my soul rejoiced. "Love not the world", it is said in the Gospel of St John. But then our Father Superior died, and a new one was appointed, a real general in a cassock. He was a ruffian and a parasite. He didn't observe the fasts. The one thing he did know about was how to conduct the services correctly, in full, strictly, and he seemed to be putting his heart into that. But he oppressed us so much that eventually the brothers would tolerate no more. Then on one of the most joyous holidays of the year, the Sunday of mutual forgiveness before Lent, when everybody should beg forgiveness of everybody else, asking for pardon and kissing with Christ in their hearts, he tore into our deacon. The man had sung something wrong in the service or made some other mistake. He buffeted his ear so hard that the deacon went flying and fell to the floor. Our cup had overflowed. The monks fell about him with their fists; but what was that to him? He roared like a wild aurochs, broke one poor monk's arm and cracked the ribs of two others; but they twisted his arms behind his back and, may God forgive us, stabbed him till he bled with the liturgical lancets used for cutting the flesh of the Holy Lamb out of communion bread. He ended up in hospital.

He got better, and came back worse than ever. You couldn't breathe. We thought it was the end. There was unrest in the monastery; the local Christian people were in uproar, knowing all about it. It was a complete scandal. The whole thing went as far as the Synod, and they cast out Herod and packed him off to the back of beyond as a bishop. Before long the howling of his new congregation could be heard in heaven.

They removed him from there and made him a penitent: now he was a simple monk again. And do you suppose that is the end of the story? Not at all. We suddenly get a letter many pages long. "Beloved brothers, forgive me, a sinner..." It was so beautifully written that many were reduced to tears. It was written with his heart's blood. He begged to be accepted back into the monastery, even as a simple monk, even as a janitor stoking the stove, anything, just so long as he could return to the monastery. He could not bear to live any longer in the world.

Meanwhile we had had our general replaced by an intellectual Father Superior, a highly educated man who had lived abroad, very wise but somehow as a result of all that knowledge very, very quiet. And nobody had any respect for him! The women would be crowded in the square and he would pass through and beg the pardon of anyone he bumped against. No, it used to be that if the old one barked at them they all fell to their knees: he kept the fear of God in them! So this way was no good either.

It all began to get to me and I left, without asking permission, and these five years I have been praying to God to forgive me the sin of pride. In the Epistle of St John it is also written that "God sent his only begotten Son into the world, that we might live through him." He loved the world, that is the

170

miracle; that is what I have come to understand here at last! But I shall go back, I shall go back soon and shall serve Him together with everyone. I have been indulging my vanity in solitude long enough. I wanted, I don't deny it, to become a saint, but what kind of saint am I? No one is more sinful in terms of our life here below. Those who have learned to endure, those are the real saints. The Church knows that well enough!

You think you should live in the forest? No, you and I must go out into the world: you to your mother, first and foremost to your own mother, and I to my other mother, the Church; and we must both beg forgiveness with tears in our eyes. And we will find forgiveness, because they love us, deep in their hearts they love us, and the rest is just chaff on the surface, foolishness born of weakness, like mushrooms springing from mould."

Father Innokenty suddenly jumped up and, in a quite different tone of voice, commanded,

"Arise, Boy, arise! Be not afraid, cast out all fear. Christ will not leave us. Let us go to pray!"

In the chapel he prayed long. Skunk did not join in, but perched silently on the bench, quietly sucking his thumb, gazing at the flickering candle stump until, without noticing, he fell asleep. Father Innokenty did not scold him, but woke him carefully and took him to the cabin to sleep, and in the morning did not constrain him. This became the established pattern: Skunk could come in to the chapel when he wanted; and if he could not or did not want to, that too seemed to be fine by the monk.

9

Winter set in almost unnoticed, and when the snow finally lay they set off to the village for provisions. They left early, in the twilight before dawn, each hauling a long, light wooden sleigh, having donned a special canvas harness. Skunk went first, lay

171

down the track in the snow, and the monk followed, fingering his rosary as he went and endlessly repeating the Lord's prayer.

At midday they came to a halt. They got a fire going, brewed up some tea, and for half an hour rested, looking at the fir trees heavy laden with snow, the sparkling snow all around, the long bog ahead of them overgrown with spindly aspen trees.

"Look how beautiful it is." Father Innokenty rose up in the sleigh in delight, clapped his hands, and they heard the sound echoing through the fir trees. "You can admire it just like looking at an icon, eh?"

Skunk nodded happily.

"You understand this!" The monk's rapturous face shone. "But there are people for whom the letter of the law is above the law itself. For me no comma is worth as much as this scraggy fir tree. They go on about tradition, fearful of every-thing... Take this forest, for instance, what colour is it basically?"

"Green, of course."

"Exactly. It is green. As the icon painters appreciated long ago. Back in the sixteenth century, when people tried harder to understand mysteries, they ventured to clothe John the Baptist in green. Who was he? A man living in the wilderness who, the scriptures tell us, was clad in a yellow camel hair shirt. Why do you think he suddenly started wearing green skins in Rus? How had they come up with the idea of a beast with green fur? Answer me that!"

"I don't know." Skunk was intrigued, suspecting a trick question.

"It's very simple. In those times Russian people started going off into the forests, into new wildernesses, so what should an anchorite look like? He should wear green, of course, forest green. And did that diminish the stature of the image? Not in the slightest. They made it more accessible, and what if it was not in accordance with the scriptures, an authentic tradition was born. How, I cannot understand, how can anyone

172

not worship beauty, not fall down and pray even to this pine tree, that rock if there is manifest in it, and in that rock too, Christ our God, and if you are God-fearing, and your prayer is addressed to God, then there is nothing bad, nothing to worry about. There has been nothing pagan about this for a long time now, and traditional understanding is no worse, but also no better, than this."

Like a little child incapable of concealing its delight, Father Innokenty fell to his knees right there in the snow and prayed in gratitude. Skunk was left standing beside him. The cold was beginning to trouble him, but he did not venture to interrupt the monk. Only when he was thoroughly chilled did Innokenty get up from his knees and they went on, pressing ahead without stopping until evening, when they reached a hunter's cabin which Father Innokenty knew from earlier journeys.

The following day they set out early, and again until their midday tea the monk was taciturn, meditative, only occasionally interrupting his prayers to take command and keep them going in the right direction in accordance with forest landmarks known only to him.

They drank their tea quickly. Father Innokenty was in a hurry. "We'll soon be there now, very soon. We shall be there by evening." It was plain that he was slightly feverish at the thought of being among people again.

"You can stay behind in the village, and go from them back into the world," he suddenly said abruptly.

"No, Father, where should I go without you?"

"Where?" the monk retorted. "Into the world! You must, my son," he added, a little subdued. "You simply will not understand: a monk is other, different; but your path is back to the world. For the moment you are a colt, but very soon you will be a young stallion. All right, if not now, then soon. We shall go our separate ways. You know all the byways of Koloch now, and if we stay together... I shall never be able to tear you from my heart." He became embarrassed, and in order to cover his confusion changed his tone again. "That's enough of that. Have patience, now you will see my winter helpmeets. As soon as they knew I was a runaway, they were drawn to me. It is an age-old characteristic of ours that we love what is secret or fugitive. They know nothing about the schism in Russian Orthodoxy or when it took place. The last of their scribes died long ago. But their faith, Lord, their faith is like flint: it is frightening. Would that I had even a fraction of it. At first they were eager to bring food to me, but I forbade it. Do you think they were offended? On the contrary: it gave me more weight in their eyes. Secrets! They are like little children: life is unimaginable without secrets. If you think about it, they only need the sacraments and the law for special occasions, in order not to lapse from discipline completely. What they really need is compassion. Two or three visits like this in the course of the winter are more than enough for them. They can live a whole year afterwards on the memory. All that time God can judge them for himself!"

The village sprang up out of the forest unexpectedly: beyond a long snow-covered meadow appeared grey huts, bathhouses, sheds. Only a few of the houses were now inhabited; the rest, boarded up, were waiting their turn to be dismantled for firewood. Well hidden away, far from the nearest station and the timber operations, in earlier times an Old Believer village but now you couldn't tell what their faith was, the village was safely lost among the forests, and it seemed as if there were no roads from here to link them with the outside world, any more than there was electricity, of course. Up under the ceiling hung old-fashioned oil lamps.

They knew the monk here, and kept the fact of his existence secret. They were proud of having a secret from the authorities, and supplied him with oil, sugar, salt, and seeds gladly and without charge. They met him with a low bow, wordlessly, almost in a trance, and conducted him to a solid two-storey log hut where a bachelor lived. On both of the nights they

174

stayed there the entire population came together: four women, two old men, and somebody's retarded daughter of about forty years of age; and with mouths agape, they listened to Innokenty's sermon and then confessed, enumerating at great length all the sins they had piled up over the past year. Innokenty took confession in the upstairs summer best room, which had been scrubbed and heated red hot specially. Those waiting sat on benches downstairs, casting timid, fawning glances at Skunk, who had squeezed himself into the corner.

In the village, having barely crossed the threshold of the hut, Innokenty was transformed, and although he bowed low to each person individually, Skunk had never before seen him so stern and aloof. What must they feel at the sight of the hermit? He even felt their austere respect and veneration directed towards himself. The women took counsel for a long time before suddenly deciding and asking him in concert: "Give us your blessing, Boy!" He was so startled he almost lost the power of speech, but collected his wits and muttered severely, "I may not". They immediately left him in peace, but he heard them whispering, "There, he's taken on a disciple. He will be even more modest than the Father. He says he may not, but you can see straight away he's Father Innokenty's novice."

When all of them, again acting as one, saw the two of them on their way, accompanying them as far as the village boundary, they stood motionless, frowning and morose, as if grudging having lost another working day, and bowed again and again after them, hiding beneath a mask of meek indifference their tremendous, unique joy.

When they stopped for the night Father Innokenty asked,

"Well, did you see enough?"

"Enough. I met people like that in Stargorod." He thought of Aunt Vera.

"Of course you did. Half of Russia consists of such people. All right, let me tell you about something that happened a long time ago instead." As always he changed the subject quite straightforwardly. It was not easy to follow the thread of his thoughts.

"This was in olden times, in Siberia. A certain priest was sent to serve in some godforsaken spot like our village. He set off alone, by sleigh, but a brigand came upon him on the way and killed him. He stole his clothes, put them on, and fled in the same direction. He arrived at the remote village, and was welcomed as the priest sent to minister to them. What was he to do? He was an educated man, a fugitive perhaps or an unfrocked priest, I'm sure I don't know; only he had to stand in for the man he had killed in order that the crime should not come to light. And imagine, he carried out the offices and conducted the services for a whole year before they found him out. They shackled the criminal and packed him off to the bridewell, while in the Synod the whole theological world gathered to decide what to do. Should they, for instance, re-christen and re-marry all those whom he had christened and married? It would have been a fairly simple matter. A new priest had already been appointed there. They could instruct him to do it, and that would be that. But a certain wise monk there was who said, "If God by his providence sent that brigand to minister to the people, then His grace came down upon the murderer, and as for the murder, he will redeem that sin in the bridewell." What is it all: a circus, play-acting? In no wise. There is real understanding there. And if I minister to the seven people here, if even once or twice in the year they hear the Word of God... and are not saved, well, that is my misfortune but probably not my sin. The Lord after all will be the judge. The most important thing, as I believe, is that he will forgive them. For he loved man above all his other creation. He loved him!"

For some reason, Innokenty became flushed towards the end of his speech and was clearly suffering some inner torment. His face twisted and twitched, and tears shone in his eyes.

"Father Innokenty, what is wrong with you?" Skunk squealed in fright. The monk looked at him closely, greedily gulping for air, and suddenly wept aloud and pressed himself to Skunk's breast. "I shall not hold back from you, my son, I shall not deceive you. I am weak, powerless, but it is only love, believe me, it is love I am suffering."

For a moment his speech relapsed into an incoherent babble, but then with an effort of will he pulled himself together, wiped the tears from his eyes, and the sight of Skunk, frightened and downcast by such an unexpected turn of events, transported him into a different kind of ecstasy, and lightly embracing him, Father Innokenty laughed an infectious, cheerful laugh.

"What rubbish I am, what a fool, a muddlehead, I have quite terrified you, but there is nothing to fear, my son, nothing. It was only a moment of weakness, such as befalls us all, eh? We must be more strict on ourselves, yes? Or no?!" He playfully pulled a face. "And everything will be back to normal and settle down again. Isn't that right?"

And again they went on, hauling the sleighs with their harnesses, and Father Innokenty was collected and serious, and once more everything in his appearance instilled respect.

10

The outing invigorated both of them. Skunk now no longer feared that he would lose Father Innokenty since, if he had brought in provisions to last through to the spring, he had clearly given up all thought of leaving. That he talked constantly about doing so was not too worrying: Skunk was used by now to his inconsistencies. The monk for his part seemed to have had his spirits raised by seeing the villagers, but through the liveliness and surface cheerfulness there began to show an edginess and inability to concentrate which he tried to suppress with work, often wholly unnecessary, or with exhausting prayers of thanksgiving. They lived together, as before, in harmony, except that the winter storms, the snow and the silence again made Skunk too lazy, and now he often stayed lying in bed, gazing mindlessly into the fire.

Such was the situation on that fateful day, a day in no wise remarkable or different from other days. He lay late in bed, then prepared a meal, chopped some firewood, looking over in puzzlement to the snow-covered chapel into which Father Innokenty had disappeared early in the morning and had given no signs of life since. Dusk began to fall.

Eventually Skunk could wait no longer and went into the chapel, but it was empty. When he lit a candle he immediately noticed that the icons were missing, only the Trinity, looking forlorn, had for some reason been left on the wall, with the icon lamp beneath it.

He ran all round the little building. No snow had fallen since yesterday, and yet there were no fresh footprints. Anywhere. Skunk waited through the night, keeping the kettle warm on the stove, and a pan of food, but Father Innokenty did not appear. He tried to remember something out of the ordinary, some word, a glance; but no. The monk had gone into the chapel early, as usual, and simply vanished, as if dissolved in the forest stillness.

In the morning Skunk got ready to search: he took a supply of food and scoured the immediate vicinity. He found no footprints or ski tracks, which was not surprising since Father Innokenty's skis were still propped up against the bathhouse wall. His strength exhausted, he straggled back home late at night. The fire had gone out. There was no one there. The next day a snowstorm blew up which kept him boxed in for three days and three nights. After the snowfall any further searching would have been futile. He settled down to wait, even though he seemed to have understood that the monk had gone for good, or more exactly, had miraculously disappeared, yet still hoping for something. By the end of the second week he was beginning to think he had dreamed everything, that there never had been a Father Innokenty, an elk, tame ravens, journeys to a hidden village. Only the little icon of the Trinity remained, but now it hung above his bedhead. For some reason he was too scared to go into the empty chapel. Oddly enough, neither the ravens nor the elk re-appeared. Against that, the wood and hazel grouse, which had not wandered on to the clearing before, became thoroughly at home, and each morning when he woke he found the snow already trampled by their three-toed feet.

Finally Skunk had had enough. He prepared to leave.

Pulling an ember from the stove, he torched the house, the bathhouse, and the chapel, and without looking back got on his skis and set off back to the world. He felt totally certain that nobody would ever settle there again. Nobody. Ever.

He tried to find the village, but for all his woodsman's memory it seemed to have been swallowed up in the snow. He spent an icy night under a fir tree by his campfire, puzzling over Father Innokenty's disappearance. He was unable to come up with an answer.

In the morning, resigned to his fate, he skied to the railway halt and got on the train. He felt neither anger nor bitterness. Once again he climbed up to the top bunk, turned to the wall and silently sucked his never-failing thumb. The train travelled slowly, paying its respects to each and every halt along the way. A feeling of loneliness and misery grew ever stronger in his stomach, or perhaps it was just that he was hungry.

11

He had an arrangement with his mother that the door key stayed in a dark corner, in a crack between two bricks, but it was not there. He had to go to the shop.

He had barely entered when Raissa rushed over from behind the counter as if she had been waiting for him.

"Lord, it's Danny back at last, our own dear wandering

pilgrim, we'd given up hope. Come through, come through. Let's get you a bite to eat."

"Where's mother?" he asked with a sense of foreboding, but Aunt Raissa only rattled on, "In a minute, in a minute, Anna Ivanovna will tell you all about it..." He became deeply uneasy.

Anna Ivanovna had aged and was overweight and, as always, sitting working on a pile of invoices. When she saw who had come in, she got up and hurried over to him: "What can I say, little one: your mother is dead."

He sat down heavily on a stool without saying a word.

"He killed her, he killed her," the more hysterical Raissa shrieked. "He hit her with the iron."

"Where is he?" Skunk asked mechanically, almost coolly, except that he hid his trembling hands under the table.

"In prison, in prison, little one. He's been sentenced to death, and the judge said there could be no mercy."

"Here? In Prison Number Two?"

"No, little one, in St Petersburg, in the Kresty Prison. We had to bury Zoika for you. We held the wake for the fortieth day of her passing in your house a week ago."

He had heard what mattered. The rest, the usual womanish chatter in such cases: where would he try to get a job, did he have any ready cash, went in one ear and out the other.

"Where is the key?"

This practical question brought Anna Ivanovna back to earth. She went to the safe and produced it.

""Let's leave the boy in peace now, Raissa. Will you be all right to get home on your own?"

He nodded.

"Right then, no arguing," Anna Ivanovna at last resumed her usual commanding officer's tone. "Here is a thousand roubles. It is Zoika's money: her wages and the bonus she never received. It's not much by today's standards, but it will see you through for the moment. I'll lend you another thousand to get yourself some clothes. You can let me have it back as and when you can. After all, Zoika was one of the family. I'll come and inspect you a time or two to see how you are getting along. You can trade in the street for us if you like. I'll see you do all right out of it. Agreed?"

Firm and forthright. He thanked her and rushed to get outside.

At home everything was tidier than it had been for a long time. Evidently Raissa had done her best. Skunk sat for a time in his corner before going back out to the town.

He walked along the street churning up with his feet the slush and mud traditional at the end of winter and feeling with his whole body the disorder and chill of the weather. He bought some bread at a bakery shop, a bottle of milk and some tins of indeterminate fish at the dairy shop. The shops were looking wrecked at the end of the day and had nothing more to offer. He walked on until he came up against a smart new sign for a "Grill-Bar". Behind the window a plaster roast chicken reclined on a cardboard dish. He stared at it, unable to decide whether or not to push the door and go in.

"Sku-unk?"

Behind him stood Zhenka.

"Sku-unk?"

She seemed glad to see him.

"Where have you been? I heard your mum died," Zhenka asked in a whisper, concerned, squeezing up close to him, and without waiting for an answer, in the same tone, went on, "Are you hungry?"

He looked at her as if she was a being from another world, so totally unexpectedly had she floated up from behind his shoulder, which she was already clinging to. She seemed a little drunk and somehow not her old self at all.

"Let's go, while I've still got some money." Zhenka almost shoved him into the grill-bar, sat him down at a corner table, and ordered chicken and a bottle of vodka. Skunk did not let her pay. They ate the food, drank the drink, and Skunk promptly ordered the same again: another bottle of vodka and another chicken. He stuffed them in a plastic bag, and for some reason confidently and boldly helped Zhenka up and took her home. She was already well oiled and just kept saying, "Oooh, Skunk, if I didn't know you better..." in justification of her easy surrender. He noted the change which had come over her: Zhenka was drinking a lot and greedily. The story was only too familiar, but in spite of everything, it reassured him.

Once they were home they demolished the chicken and made short work of the vodka. Completely slewed, Zhenka kept saying, "I've got some money left. Let's run out and get another one, eh?"

But he resolutely undressed her, dragged her to his mother's broad bed, and for some reason pulled the curtain.

"Sku-unk, what am I doing? I've got a lawful wedded husband now," Zhenka murmured and tried to go to sleep, but he did not let her.

12

The first wave of inebriation had passed. He was thirsty and his throat felt as if it had been sandpapered. Skunk ran to the bathroom, lapped the rust-coloured water straight from the tap, and brought some to Zhenka in an aluminium ladle. She was amazingly loving and comfortable. He lay listening to her babble, at one moment boasting, the next complaining, completely uninhibited and going into detail as only very drunk, very kind, and very stupid people can.

"Mine is in prison now, but don't you think, you know... He really is an absolute sweetie — so, so nice! He landed up inside because of me, you know, because of his pride, his sense of honour. Because they have their own code of honour. He is a real thief, not one of your sad foreign currency touts. Remember Valyusha? She drives around in a Mercedes now. Her guy is in a joint venture company with some foreigners. Her Mercedes is crap, to tell the truth, but my guy is a real gentleman. If he says yes he'll never let you down. When he got put away, their Mr Big came round to see me and mum. He brought my favourite liqueur, and some fruit, a smoked sausage, and money, lots of it, and my favourite ciggies. They're called "Sea", lovely brown ones, do you know them? Anyway, don't you worry, he says, I'll take care of you. And every month he brings us stuff, and my guy's still got a whole year to go. Ooh-la-la!"

Skunk listened half asleep as she chattered on. Nothing seemed to irritate him now or make him angry. Idiot Zhenka went blethering on and on about the man she loved, or maybe didn't love. Skunk felt as free of care as he had in the forest, but somehow also specially warm, and everything seemed childishly funny.

Towards morning, around six o'clock, their heads finally cleared. Zhenka put on the light, got dressed, looked down at his sleepy face, and winked: "Sku-unk, fancy a chomp?" But the lightness of childhood had gone, the naive flirtation. Before him stood a grown, healthy woman, tired, not in a very good mood, and about to go off and forget all about him.

"Wait..."

"That's all we need. Thanks, Skunky, I enjoyed that, but I have to go. I have a daughter now, you know. My mother will go spare again. She's such a cow..." She did not finish the sentence, pecked his cheek, and sailed away.

13

Skunk did not stay in bed for long. An agitation the like of which he had never known (it was not anger), forced him to get up. Even a hot shower could not cure his nervous shaking. Without properly drying himself, leaving the dirty dishes and pots and pans in the kitchen and main room, he went outside.

He felt drawn past the transport depot of the fertilizer

factory, past the fish wharf, past the factory to his old pumping station. He pushed the half open door, and was assailed by the smell of a long unheated, abandoned place. The stove had collapsed and jutted up like a rotten tooth; on the walls icicles and disgusting bubbles of plaster vied for space with frozen mould. Even in the gloom his eye picked out particular outlines: a pile of old newspapers and some kind of official lists; what looked like a car tyre with damaged cording. Those had never been here before, and there was something else, revoltingly foreign and dead. He got back outside to the fresh air. Everything around was grey: the snow which hadn't yet finally melted, the chill puddles with their icy slush, the slow, sluggish river far away down below.

He was really shivering now. His teeth were chattering, his eyes hurting, as if someone were pressing in on them. The light began to fade, and the surrounding objects to blur. He wandered as if in a fog, his feet leading him to the river and the balustrade around St Andronicus's stone. He felt ill. He was developing a fever. Skunk lay down on the rock and drew up his legs. The last of the light disappeared. His head spun, he lost his usual sensations: the fever from inside, the cold weather without no longer troubled him. His body seemed covered in protective scales. Some amazingly light, pleasant medium flowed over him, perhaps a breeze or water, or perhaps it was the beating of invisible, weightless wings caressing him. With a second sight completely new to him he saw or felt something that happens only rarely on the summit of a high mountain, when a gulf is at your feet and a strong cold wind blowing straight at you from the firmament. Time rushed at him, through him, with a speed beyond the grasp of intellect. His body became weightless and rapture spread into its every corner, and all the while time was rushing, rushing, until suddenly it vanished.

The next morning three old women came to the rock. From a distance they decided that the sacred relic had been profaned by some city lout, and hastened towards it at a trot, but when they came nearer, they slowed down and then came completely to a halt at the balustrade. The poor women looked around them helplessly, but there was nobody near, and then, without a word among themselves, they started wailing, "The rock, the rock: it's hovering in the air." Only when the boulder sank smoothly back down on to the ground did they dare to go through the gate, but then again stopped short.

"Holy saints, if it isn't Danny Khoryov," the churchwarden recognized the body lying there. "It's Danny, my dears, and the breath quite gone from his body. God forgive us, it has been granted us to see Thy miracle."

"Look, look! He has been crying, he has been crying," another pointed trembling to the wet streaks on his serene, untroubled, smiling face.

The women made the sign of the Cross and then, as one, rushed to the church for help.

But when they came back with a whole procession of priests and the deacon and a crowd of other old women, the stone was empty. Father Boris with his cropped head told the women off at great length, and stout Father Trifon questioned them in detail, but they were not to be dissuaded of what they had seen. And no one in Stargorod ever saw Danny the Skunk again.

Epilogue

Skunk recovered from his miraculous blackout and left Stargorod. He wandered north again by the route familiar to him and came to a stop in the village where once he had stolen the shotgun. He was taken on in the local timber factory by a lady some years his elder, divorced but still lively, and she set him to work the power-saw.

As a result of some madness which no one had known about, this gloomy oddity soon married his unattractive partner

185

in a distant church and got himself a new identity document, taking his wife's surname. He was now registered as Daniil Anastasiev, but known among the village people as Sonya's man, in honour of the woman who had appropriated him. The nickname stuck, and he grew used to it.

Sonya's Daniil has an easy life, knocks his already pregnant wife about a bit, and threatens from time to time to run away from her and become a forester, where the pay is better. His wife, understandably, howls at this, but also reckons that a few extra roubles would not come amiss in these fast-moving times. In her heart she knows that her brooding little husband, who is so gentle with her in bed, only really finds fulfilment in the forest.

On summer evenings Sonya's man often sits on the logs piled by the fence, looking at the nearby forest, half-listening to the women gossiping by the well. In the newly re-opened Klopsky Monastery a preacher and confessor of extraordinary compassion has appeared, a healer who has emerged from a strict twenty year long retreat in the forest. Popular opinion has already declared the monk a saint, and the women keep meaning to go together to see him. He hears also about the miraculous shining of St Andronicus's stone in faraway Stargorod which portends the imminent end of the world, and about the neighbour's boar which has been cut down by an evil spell, about how prices keep going up and up, and about the misdeeds of the authorities in Moscow. He smiles wryly into the wispy beard he has grown.

Sonya's man rarely drinks hooch with the other men, but when he does he becomes unpredictably pugnacious, frightening, and revoltingly lustful. On these occasions Sonya runs away to spend the night with a lady neighbour. He is not a prey to drinking bouts, however, always apologizes in the morning, and takes his hangover off into the stillness of the forest, disappearing somewhere and returning towards night the same as he was before he got drunk.

1990-93

Our century's brilliant literary magician

Here at last is the definitive Nabokov collection, capturing as never before both the breadth and brilliance of his American period. His autobiography and eight novels published 1941-1974 are collected for the first time in this authoritative set, newly edited to incorporate Nabokov's handwritten corrections. The first volume includes *The Real Life of Sebastian Knight*; *Bend Sinister*; *Speak, Memory*. Volume two features *Lolita*; *Pnin*; *Pale Fire*; *Lolita: A Screenplay*. In the final volume: *Ada, or Ardor*; *Transparent Things*; *Look at the Harlequins!*

Photo by Philippe Halsman ©Halsman Estate

editor: Brian Boyd

A Shrimp *Learnt* to Whistle

A Shrimp Learnt to Whistle is unlike any other book on post-Soviet Russia. Why? Because the author is a British journalist who has lived Russia for extended periods on a Russian salary, independently, witho the benefit of exclusive accommodation and an expense account. Sara Hurst followed up her studies in Russia by becoming a staff reporter *The St Petersburg Press* (now *The St Petersburg Times*) in 1995-96, during the Duma election and the run-up to the presidential election.

A Shrimp Learnt to Whistle is about Russian life from the inside. It contains a huge number of poignant, shocking and humorous intervie with people as diverse as Kolya Vasin, the founder of St Petersburg's John Lennon Temple of Peace and Love, and the late Mikhail Botvinnik, world chess champion under Stalin. Grigory Yavlinsky an Galina Starovoitova are amongst the present-day politicians interview in the book.

A Shrimp Learnt to Whistle is available only by mail order from Elephant Publishing. The price is £6.95 + £1.25 p&p within the UK, in Europe or £4 for the rest of the world. Customers outside the Uk should pay by banker's draft. Please make cheques payable to Elepha Publishing. Allow 28 days for delivery.

Elephant Publishing

33 Elvendon Road, Goring-on-Thames, Near Reading, RG8 ODP
Tel/fax: (01491) 873227   e-mail: rivervalley@easynet.co.uk

S L A V O N I C A

— A New Series of Scottish Slavonic Review —

A twice-yearly publication on the languages, literatures, history and culture of Russia and Central & Eastern Europe

Contents of this issue include

plus review articles and book reviews, obituaries and reports

Submissions and editorial enquires

The Editor, S L A V O N I C A
Department of Russian Studies
The University of Manchester
Oxford Road
Manchester M13 9PL
Tel 0161-275 3138 Fax 0161-275 33031
e-mail: russian@manchester.ac.uk

Subscriptions and business inquiries, books and periodicals for review

Please send to the address above

Modern Poetry in Translation

An international journal

No 10: Russian Poetry

Akhmatova, Aranzon, Aygi, Bukharaev,
Khlebnikov, Khodasevich, Ivanov,
Parnok, Rein, Tarkovsky, Tsvetayeva,
Voznesensky, Zugman & others,
+ Peter Levi on translating poetry
+ reviews, articles
+ a feature on Joseph Brodsky

Back issues still available:
Bonnefoy, FB Steiner, Kamieńska, Jerusalem Festival, Galician-
Portuguese troubadours, Brazil, Wales, France, Filipino poetry

No 11: Peru & more Russian poetry

Single issues (190-240 pages): £9.50 (UK/EU) | $18 (Overseas) postfree
Subscriptions (2 issues per annum) pro rata
(Cheques payable to King's College London, please)

Details from *Norma Rinsler*,
MPT, King's College London, Strand, London WC2R 2LS

FUNDED BY THE ARTS COUNCIL OF ENGLAND

New Books   **Used Books**

Shakespeare and Company
MOSCOW

In the Paris tradition of Sylvia Beach, Henry Miller,
James Joyce, Andre Gide and Anais Nin, we invite you
to visit our cheery, petite basement abode.
A wide selection of new and used books are available
for your reading pleasure.

Welcome to our weekly "Literary Saturdays" where
Russian authors read from their new works, in Russian and
English, followed by discussions and socializing.

*Shakespeare & Company
Moscow
was founded on
1 April 1996
by
Mary R. Duncan,
an American Professor
at San Diego
State University,
and
Alexander Ivanov,
the Director of
Ad Marginem Press.*

*Address:
1st Novokuznetsky per.
5/7, Moscow, Russia
tel: (7095) 231 9360*